JUDE

by

CHRISTINE B. BEST

JUDE

Author: Christine B. Best

Copyright © 2015 Nissi Publishing, Inc.

Nissi Publishing, Inc.
Roanoke, TX

Printed in the United States of America.

ISBN: 978-0-944372-24-1

Table of Contents

Acknowledgements

I would love to thank my wonderful husband, Michael, and our sons, Justin Blevins and Samuel Best. They were truly my inspiration! I would also like to thank my family and friends and FB readers who held me to the finish of my beloved JUDE! Last, but not least, my wonderful editor, Joyce, and my two friends named Sherry who gave me the courage to put it out there, as well as my author friend, Leslie.

Chapter 1

A Funeral

The crisp breath of early fall blew lazily through the neat row of headstones in the Eternal Rest Cemetery. The grey clouds were hovering just above the green tent as the last bars of "Amazing Grace" were being sung. The soprano voice of Mary Lloyd, from the church choir, pierced the thick, heavy air of grief. *"Dust to dust, ashes to ashes,"* the minister spoke in a monotone voice foretelling of brighter days to come. He concluded the service and invited family and friends to come by and pay their last respects to the ones seated in the velvet-covered folding chairs. The slight chill in the air propelled the mourners to huddle closer together as they each waited their turn to pass by the family.

Jude was still in the fog that encompasses sudden death. The unthinkable had happened. There hadn't been time to process what it all meant. After all, it had only been four days since she had received the life-shattering news of her husband's fatal car crash.

Just hours before the police called, Grayson, her husband, woke up with food on his mind. "What's for dinner tonight?" he whispered, brushing a good morning kiss on her forehead. "I'm not working late, so we can be on time to your friend's surprise party. I'm not much on cucumber sandwiches or sausage crepes though." They both snickered as he rubbed a foreseen bellyache.

"I'll make us a spinach salad," she said. "Oh, and with that grilled chicken the way you like it," she told him in her still sleepy voice.

"Man, I love that salad dressing you make with it," he said. *That was it. Or was it? Did he actually say, "Sounds good," or did he say that part first? Or was it, "I want that dressing"? Or was it the other way around?* If she would have known it was the last time to ever hear his voice, she would have listened more intently.

Jude snapped out of her daze as Aunt Myrtle, in her long black dress and 1960's back comb, leaned over, offering her condolences, the sweet smell of peppermint on her breath. Over her shoulder, Jude caught a glimpse of a beautiful redbird clutching the branch of a dormant oak tree.

The line filed quietly by, each one whispering heartfelt sentiments, until she was finally able to stand to her feet. The creaking and groaning of the device which lowered the casket sent an eerie chill down her spine. She, along with her son and daughter, watched in disbelief. *Is this it? Is this really the last time to be a whole family?*

Jude Mitlow, a tall, beautiful woman, carried herself with an air of class that made people notice her. Today, she had her long, brunette hair pulled into a French twist. Her swollen eyes were partially obscured by the short, black netting attached to her vintage pillbox hat that had belonged to her mother. Her sharp features accented pretty green eyes and full lips. She looked great, albeit the occasion was a funeral. Her 49th birthday had come and gone. She had no problem with the tiny lines around her eyes or the silver streak at her left temple her hairdresser continued to battle. She had often said the tiny lines marked her "rite of passage." The hair—well that was easily remedied.

She had chosen a black designer dress for today. The only jewelry she wore was her wedding ring and the classic strand of pearls he had given her years ago on their 10th wedding anniversary. Shiny black pumps and an ecru lace handkerchief completed her outfit. She was "put together" for this horrible day marking the end of her near-perfect marriage of 31 years to Grayson Mitlow. Her children hovered protectively on either side of her and helped her into the waiting silver limo reserved for grieving families. Her son, Jackson, 29 years old, clutched her waist. Even with his big frame and optimistic personality he was blinded with grief. Jessica, the younger of the two by one year to the day, remained quiet and reserved, staring outside the window. Numb, lost in her thoughts, Jude looked down through blurry eyes at the two sets of hands clutching hers. She barely noticed the limo slowly making its way out of the cemetery.

Jude adored her children and had sacrificed her own career long ago when they were born. Even though both were grown and had moved away, she still enjoyed staying home. With all the upheaval in the world and small pockets of civil wars exploding in every country, Grayson had been more comfortable with her being at home. Her education was in mortuary services—dead bodies. She loved to do makeup and hair at a local funeral home, but only as time had allowed it; her family came first. She enjoyed her free-lance work when the funeral home needed her and her occasional volunteer work at church.

Life was good with Grayson's successful partnership at the Mitlow and Ferguson Law Firm. Even in the middle of political uprisings and scattered terrorist attacks on the United States and embassies worldwide, the business had continued to flourish; people still needed legal services.

She had no clue on how to get through the rest of the day, much less tomorrow. *How could this have happened? My husband, best friend and partner—gone.* Jude could almost hear his voice coming through the heavy, consuming pain in her heart telling her even now to *"Keep moving forward, Jude. God's plan is always perfect."*

Jude knew Jackson would be there for her; he lived close. He owned a small gym up the road and still ate most of his meals at her home. Jessica, just getting her law practice off the ground, was always at the courthouse. *What would become of her now with Grayson gone?*

The ride in the limo was long and silent—each person held captive by their own thoughts. Out of nowhere, the limo driver was extending his hand, helping her out of the car, and once again, she was ushered through another door. At least this one was familiar; she was home, finally. Colleyville suburbia: big brick homes, scattered Italian stuccos, HOAs, the guard gate—the life they enjoyed.

The caterer's car and florist vans were parked on one side of the driveway. People had already begun to gather and covered dishes, mainly casseroles and pies, were being brought in by concerned neighbors and church family. The Mitlows were loved by many people. Two dozen cars lined both sides of the street, crippling thru traffic.

Jude went upstairs to her room to get a moment alone and change clothes. She needed a break from the well-meaning crowd.

She slipped out of the funeral suit and dropped it into the now overfilled dry-cleaning bin on her way out of the bathroom. Time had stood still. She stopped long enough to pick up one of his T-shirts, still slung over a dressing chair, and pressed it to her face, inhaling the lingering, timeless scent he'd worn for years. "Oh, Grayson," she whispered quietly.

She was slipping into her slacks and sweater when Jessica appeared with a hot cup of coffee. "Here, Mother. Just another hour or so and everyone will go home. Then you can put your yoga pants back on. Jackson and I will stay as long as you need us to. I know you're ready to be alone. Just hang in there. We'll figure it all out."

Jude looked at her daughter's brown eyes—Grayson's eyes, but red and puffy. Jude slipped her arm around her and gave her a hug, although Jessica wasn't usually the "touchy-feely" type. "I know you keep things in, Jessica. We're here for you. We'll get through this as a family."

Jessica unconsciously shrugged her mother's arm off of her shoulder. "Jackson said he'd stay here with you for a while if you need him to," she said.

As if Jude didn't notice the non-verbal action, she responded, "We have plenty of time to figure all that out. Let's just get through the next few days." She brushed a loose strand of hair from her daughter's face and tucked it behind her ear.

"Well," Jessica said, standing up straighter, "you know I would stay, too, but it's such a long commute from downtown Dallas."

"I wouldn't hear of it anyway," Jude said. "I'm gonna get through this. I'm fine. You have your new office to get up and running. Your brother is close by. We'll get everything sorted out."

"Well, I'm handling all of the legal stuff," stated Jessica, as she slipped on her own comfy shoes. "When I opened my private practice, Dad gave me copies of all of your important papers like the will, the deed to the house, stocks, investments and everything else—just in case this very thing ever happened. I haven't gone over everything yet, of course, but I've got your entire portfolio. I know how to do this, Mother. You don't have to worry about a thing. Dad left you set. Jackson does his thing; I'll do mine," she said, putting both hands out at arm's length for emphasis.

"I know you're a good lawyer," Jude said, one eyebrow raised, but you're also a girl who just lost her father."

"I can handle it," Jessica said.

Jackson poked his bald head in the door as if on cue. Jude's eyes darted instantly to his. "Guys, y'all come on downstairs," he motioned with his head as he took Jude by the hand. "The sooner they see you, the sooner they'll go home. Just think, yoga pants, hot tea …. You can do this, Mom, come on."

Jackson, well over 6 ft., has muscles on muscles. Working in the fitness business, at 260 lbs., his arms are now the size of his thighs. His lips are full like his mother's, and he has her emerald green eyes (both inheriting them from the Barnard side of the family—Jude's family). He's a serious type, not easily excitable, never in a hurry and extremely laid back. He loves his customers. He even built an upscale flat above the gym for convenience. He's also an all-white and stainless steel guy—ultra modern—white sofas, white carpet. The only color is a splash of blue in the form of a throw pillow and a rug (Jude's idea).

His gym is located in the heart of the city, close to his parents' home. He designed his flat with one-way glass so he could keep an eye on things in the gym. Sometimes on the weekends, Jessica would stay with him just to "dirty it up" as he accused her. She claimed it was to make sure things were running smoothly as she could observe through the glass. Nosy is what Jackson called it, but he indulged the lawyer side of her. He's crazy about his sister. She can be scrappy, but he loves that about her.

In contrast to his large size and baldness, Jessica has her mother's long, dark hair and slender build. She's lanky, with above average height. Like Jackson, she is relatively quiet, but with a great sense of humor—until she enters the courtroom. Then she, too, becomes a force to be reckoned with. She lives in Dallas close to her office in an upper-class apartment, but she's never really there. Most of her things are still in boxes. No white couches here. She's an outdoor girl and could care less about any frou-frou. Jude teased Jessica that if she had her choice, she would live in a hammock.

Two healthy, confident children and Jude and Grayson couldn't have been more proud. The only perceived flaw is the sometimes strained relationship between Jude and her daughter, but no family is perfect. Jessica has always been a little envious of her mother and brother's closeness. Jude said it was her imagination, but with his childhood asthma and constant need for care at home, it was no wonder. When he turned 14, the asthma disappeared—the heart-to-heart connection remained. She loved her daughter equally, but she could never convince Jessica of that. Jessica was content with her adult relationship with her mother; they had found their way, as mother and daughter relationships go. Jessica understood early on that Jackson would always be close by like her mother's own guardian angel.

They all headed toward the stairs when Jackson stopped and looked around. "Don't eat any of the peach pie or Mexican casserole."

"What?" Jude asked, crinkling her nose, the comment temporarily catching her off guard.

"Mom," Jessica chimed in, "we know Ms. Lou brought them. I stood guard until she wrote her name on the dish." They nearly all got tickled for one inappropriate moment.

"Shhhhhhh," cautioned Jude, with her perfectly manicured finger, "she might hear you."

"Well, you don't like to eat any of her stuff because of that cat in her house," Jackson whispered. Jude stopped.

"Please, guys, for Pete's sake, what if somebody hears us? It would hurt her feelings. But," she concurred, "I happen to know for a fact," she wagged with her shushing finger, "she lets that cat sit on her countertop while she's in the kitchen. I don't want my pie crust rolled where a cat has been sitting."

"Mother!" Jessica whisper-shouted, glancing down the staircase, "we sound like terrible, ungrateful people."

They wiped the grins off of their faces and got serious again as they joined their guests.

Night finally came. All the guests had gone home, casseroles had been put away in the freezer, and Jude had taken a long, hot bath. The kids were downstairs drinking iced tea and sorting through old photo albums, laughing one minute, crying the next. The "day of all days" was finally coming to an end. Standing by the bed, she took the decorative pillows off and tossed them into an overstuffed, cream-colored chair and folded the silver duvet. She stared into the darkness to his side of the bed. She had survived the day with God's help and her loving children by her side. She had made it through, but tomorrow—all the new tomorrows—how would she do it? *"One foot in front of the other, that's how,"* she thought. Jude was a strong woman; she could face whatever life had waiting for her.

Chapter 2

And So It Begins

It had been nearly seven weeks since the funeral. Fall had turned to crisp, cool mornings, and the hint of a cold winter lay just ahead. The lawns were still dotted with a few scraggily late blooms, and the trees were finally releasing the remainder of their once glorious red leaves to drop—brown and lifeless.

Jude, still in her white chenille robe, was curled up on the sofa in the den having her second cup of morning coffee. A cozy fire blazed in the hearth as she watched the news, her hair wadded up in a bling-bling clip. Wars were raging hotter than ever in the Middle East. Just days after Grayson's graveside service, things had changed rapidly, heating up to the boiling point in the desert. Iran had begun firing at Israel—Israel firing back. America was just sitting on its haunches doing nothing to help.

Things were escalating like never before. Not just in the Middle East; the border of Texas and Mexico had been closed after beheadings ensued with the arrival of multiple bands of terrorists. The lines had been drawn. The border stations were crawling with ISIS cell pods set up for miles after a full-on march across South America, up through the heart of Mexico. The Mexican Militia were fighting with all they had while the world stood blindly by, watching ISIS gain power, momentum and numbers. They couldn't stop this army—it seemed nobody could. No more coming across at will. No more amnesty. It didn't matter which side of the issue they came down on at this point. Nobody wanted their heads cut off. Texas' side was heavily armed with drones, tanks, artillery and ground power. Tensions were rising daily, but they hadn't made it across—not yet. The heavy, choking smoke filled the air for miles on both sides of the proverbial fence making it difficult to see. Machine guns blasting off one minute; isolated explosions the next. With all the confusion and smoke, even those using infrared binoculars were having a difficult time seeing the enemy in their black garb. They could cross at any moment.

Jackson came out of the downstairs guest room (formally his room growing up), barefoot and in black gym shorts. He headed for the kitchen. Jude glanced up momentarily to admire all the colorful tattoos and the towel slung around his neck from a fresh shower. He had completely moved back in with her. She once again became engrossed in what was happening on the television while he poured himself a cup of coffee, swallowed two raw eggs and headed into the den to join her. "Your friend's on the window sill." They both glanced over to a tree limb that hung close to the window, and Jude saw the beautiful cardinal. He seemed to go everywhere she did.

She had told her children as they were growing up, that redbirds reminded her of God. "No matter where you are, no matter how bleak the situation," she'd told them, "just look at the redbird. He neither sows or reaps but is provided for and protected by the Master. He remains beautiful and constant during any circumstance, like beauty among ashes."

"Seriously?" he questioned, looking at the upheaval on the 60-inch flat screen. He sat down and nudged her feet over. "This early in the morning, Ma? What's going on?"

"You tell me," she answered. "You and your dad have kept up with this stuff more than I have." Her thoughts trailed off thinking about his and Grayson's "secret meetings" in the study and all of those weekend hunting trips.

"Mom, this looks like it's getting even more serious, not to mention closer to home. There are things Dad didn't want you to worry about, but he's gone. This situation is going to continue to escalate. We need to talk about a game plan for safety in case we need to get out of here in a hurry."

"What?" Jude put the TV on pause, her hand covering her heart. "What are you talking about? Our safety? They've closed the borders, son," she said, looking up over her TV glasses. "Unless you're referring to something else. Is that what you're saying? Like nukes? Our homes destroyed?" she said with her voice getting higher and higher.

"Mother, calm down," he said, putting his hand on her shoulder. "I'm not talking about going underground right this minute. But you know the Scriptures as well as any of us. You know what's coming. Dad and I just think it's here—or Dad and I *thought* ...." He paused mid-sentence. "It's still hard to grasp that he's not here," he said, momentarily getting lost in that thought.

Jude stared at her son in agreement. "I know. It's been nearly two months. It still doesn't seem possible."

"Yeah," he said, "sometimes I can't help but think where exactly is he? I know he's with the Lord; he was saved, but where EXACTLY with the Lord is he? It just feels like he disappeared."

"I know," agreed Jude, patting his knee.

She unpaused the TV. All at once, more chaos erupted. "Oh, no!" Jude shouted. "They just shot that man right in front of the camera!"

Jackson grabbed the remote from her and punched up the volume. They both scooted up on the edge of the sofa watching the horror unfold in front of them. Blood and matter spattered across the cameraman's lens. They both shrank back in disbelief. Jackson's coffee sloshed out of the cup onto his hands. Another shot rang out. Pandemonium was spreading. People were beginning to panic, trampling over each other, trying to get out of the line of fire. The cameraman, trying to keep up, couldn't keep the camera still. It was bouncing up and down. He ran breathlessly, trying to report play by play of the terrorist attack on yet another U.S. Embassy.

A foreign language, gibberish, the all-in-black militia, appeared out of nowhere. Although it was in the Middle East, our troops blended in with the crowd through the fire and smoke. On the big screen, it felt like the shooting was right there in their living room—like they needed to take cover as well. The bullets whizzed around everywhere, whistling as they hit their marks. The cameraman dropped his camera, being assaulted and dragged to the ground while the film rolled. His terrified face, now on the ground, lay just inches from the cracked lens.

The phone rang loudly, and a vibrating sound came from the pocket of Jackson's gym shorts. They both nearly jumped out of their skins. Jackson grabbed his earpiece and hit the answer button, nearly shoving it into his ear canal. "Jessica, you need to get to Mom's now," he said firmly. "No, I mean leave right now! Okay, be careful," he answered in the one-sided conversation with Jude listening intently. "Wrap it up. Yes, we're watching, too. Another embassy; everybody captured and dragged out into the streets. God only knows what's happening to them."

"She's locking up now," he said to his mother, clicking off the earpiece. "She's closing the office."

"Oh, thank goodness," said Jude, with drawn eyebrows. "She needs to come home."

"She said it was pretty scary this morning on her way to the office. The military was all over the place. It looked like they were setting up patrol pods."

"Patrol pods?" questioned Jude. "Patrolling who?"

The TV scrambled for what seemed like forever, then came back on with a cheerful commercial on how to achieve softer laundry. "How odd," remarked Jude, looking over at Jackson.

"Indeed," he agreed, "extremely odd."

Chapter 3

Plus or Minus

Jude was in the kitchen putting the finishing touches on dinner. The smell of bread baking in the oven permeated the room. Jessica came in the front door, announcing her arrival as she plunked a huge suitcase and two briefcases on the floor. Jackson scooted the heavy piece of luggage out of the way with his foot and set the black leather cases on the countertop. "What's all that?" asked Jude, wiping her hands on her apron. "And what took you so long? We tried to call you."

"It's just a few things," Jessica said, looking over at the pale pink suitcase. "I went by the apartment to grab some clothes. I'm going to stay here for a while, with all of this going on." She splayed her hands. "There was another Anti-war protest right in front of the courthouse this morning. All that screaming, flags burning. Then the Pro-war groups were throwing rocks trying to save the flag. It was awful! I'm scared to go to work; scared about going home. And that's just not me. I've never been afraid of anything; however, I will admit since Tony and I separated last year, I've just never gotten comfortable living by myself again, especially now."

Jude looked up at Jackson, surprised, then back at Jessica. "I thought we weren't supposed to mention his name."

"You're not," Jessica assured her, "I brought him up. I didn't want to mention him either, but you need to know. He came by a few weeks ago—six to be exact—right after Dad passed away. He was here on leave from that military cult thingy he's involved in. He spent the night. So, yeah, you could say I've 'seen' him. He was just in for the weekend, about to go back for another tour of duty," she said, shaking a regretful head. "I don't know what I was thinking. I mean legally we *ARE* still married, even if he doesn't acknowledge it. And he was acting very odd," she added, sounding perplexed.

"Oh, dear," said Jude, catching on quick to the implication. She didn't know what to say. Jackson just shook his head.

"He made his choice, Jessica. Seems like you finally started getting your life back on track."

"Stop. I know how you both feel about him, but guys," she warned, putting both hands out as if to stop their words, "there's more. I mean there MAY be more, so don't say anything you can't take back. I not only stopped by the house to get a few of my clothes, I stopped by the drugstore and got a pregnancy test—you know, the kind you use at home?" She just blurted it out. You could have heard a pin drop. Jude was stunned at the words. She couldn't speak. She just stared dumbfounded at the oven mitts she was still wearing.

"And?" inquired Jackson, eyebrows raised sky high.

"Well, I haven't peed on it yet," she said, folding her arms in front of her waist. "I think you're supposed to do it in the morning—and stop looking at my stomach!" He looked away. Nobody uttered a word. This news couldn't have come at a worse time. "Anyway y'all," she said, letting out a big exasperated sigh, "my car's been dinged twice with the flying rocks. The only place I feel safe is here. I've got this eerie feeling the terrorists are getting closer and closer. I brought enough clothes for the rest of the week."

Jude squinted her eyes as she glanced down at Jessica's stomach again as if she might see something she had obviously missed before. Jackson put a heavy arm on his sister's shoulder. "Well, I guarantee I'll take care of you, Jessica. You'll be safe here."

"I know you'd stand between me and anybody, but Jackson, even you can't stop a bullet or a machete. What if there's a kid? What was I even thinking?!" Nobody bothered to answer that rhetorical question as she turned and went upstairs to grab a quick shower before dinner.

Jude was taking the bread out of the oven, still feeling dazed, while Jackson was helping himself to another spoonful of the chicken spaghetti cooling on the countertop. Jude's thoughts drifted once again to the poor cameraman and how the whole world seemed to be falling apart, including their family. *"What if the pregnancy test is positive? This is no time to bring a baby into the world. But if there is one, it's my grandbaby. Poor Jessica,"* thought Jude, *"she had finally accepted her short-lived marriage was over, lost her father and now this."* She could just ring Tony's neck. He should have stayed gone.

A quarter of an hour later, Jessica came downstairs in only a long, white T-shirt and short shorts, towel-drying her wet hair as if nothing had changed.

"Dude," said Jackson, looking at her supposed "lack of pants," "we don't need to see all that."

"Get over it, tattoo boy. I'm wearing shorts under here," she said, while she grabbed the tea glasses and started filling them with ice.

Jackson crinkled his nose in fake disgust.

"Well, that makes us all feel a little better," said Jude, shaking her head. They all moved the dishes to the formal dining room. It was completely Jude—vintage; beige, covered chairs; massive chandelier. They all sat down, joined hands like they had done a thousand times, and said the blessing, holding each other's hands a little more tightly. They filled their plates while their minds drifted in and out of wars and rumors of war and babies.

Chapter 4

A Baby and a Bullet

Jude padded slowly down the stairs as dawn was just beginning to break. It was glorious. The brilliance of pink, gold and purples came crashing through the wall of windows overlooking the den. She could barely take her eyes away from it. She thought daybreak was always so hopeful. Just outside the dining room doors lay a beautiful garden patio with wind chimes of every kind, gently moving in the morning breeze. Her morning routine consisted of coffee and the garden. She would fill her cup, then the backyard bird feeders. Most of them were miniature replicas of white-washed church houses. The blue jays and redbirds gathered daily along with the mourning doves and sparrows. She loved them all. Next, she fiddled with the hanging baskets overflowing with mounds of purple petunias. She meandered around the patio making mental notes to water this one, re-pot that one and really just enjoy the general splendor that only morning brings. After that, she went back indoors. She grabbed her second cup of coffee, hurried through her Bible reading and sat in the den waiting—waiting for Jessica to hurry up and go to the bathroom.

While Jessica was growing up, she was an easy kid. She didn't get into trouble and naturally made good grades. Stubborn. A little opinionated, but never petty. She was a joy. She hadn't shown any real interest in boys until she was around fifteen, and then, just a vague curiosity. Jude was remembering all the details of the last 30 years in light of yesterday's news.

Jessica was a late bloomer, but once she graduated high school and had most of her law classes behind her, she had met the infamous Tony at a local coffeehouse. He was tall, good-looking, blonde—essentially, the whole package. He swept her off her feet. They were married before Jude and Grayson could even spell his last name, Gargentella, which

Jessica being Jessica hadn't even taken or hyphenated with her name. She was a Mitlow. They had a decent time—at least for a while. But he had his sights set on an odd new branch of the Combined Armed Forces Agency, better known as CAFA. He had made that clear from the beginning. But as young love goes, nobody was listening. They had been okay for a couple of years. Then his longing turned into bitter resentment. That, coupled with his preoccupation with world peace and off-the-wall religious views, changed him to no longer be the same guy. After a while, he had come in and announced he wanted a divorce and had joined the Special Ops part of CAFA. And that was it. He never even officially filed for legal separation; he just left. It was about a year before Grayson had passed since they had heard anything from him; Jessica had always been very private about their relationship until now. Nobody liked him. He had proven to be a great disappointment.

It was hard for Jude to patiently wait for her to wake up. What she wanted to do was to walk in there and demand that Jessica get up and pee on the stick while Jude tapped her foot in the hallway until they had a plus or minus sign, but she restrained herself.

Jackson joined her in the den and was finishing off his first cup of coffee with feigned interest in the muted TV program while Jessica slowly made her way down the stairs looking at the plastic stick she was carrying. They both looked up wordlessly, wondering if she was going to bring it into the den. They could tell by the look on her face it must be sporting a plus sign. "So, does this mean I can't drink coffee anymore?" inquired Jessica, waving the stick.

"Well, I drank coffee when I carried both of you," Jude instantly remarked, never missing a beat. "In moderation, of course. But I think that's fine." She was so proud of herself. She had played it cool like she rehearsed in her mind. She wanted to say something clever, but all she could come up with was her ability to drink coffee while pregnant, thirty something years ago. Brilliant.

Jackson, shielding his cup from the stick Jessica was waving around, made light of the proclamation. "Well, go on and get that cup of coffee," he said, motioning her toward the kitchen. "Just because you have a 4-centimeter embryo in your …"

"womb" (Jude helped him to finish his sentence).

"What she said," Jackson continued, "we're not going to start waiting on you hand and foot."

They all laughed, knowing he was teasing, but it also served to break up the tension and pretend Jude hadn't used the "w" word. It grossed them both out when she used the correct anatomical words for sensitive conversations like they were thirteen again, getting "the talk."

One thing their family prided themselves in was, when the going became difficult, they had the ability to move forward. After all, they now had a baby on the way to love and adore.

Jessica brought her coffee in the den as well, and they all settled in to watch the news to see what all had transpired since yesterday. Jude unmuted the TV, and the broadcast had already started. "… on the steps of a Dallas courthouse yesterday afternoon," said the pretty blonde anchorwoman. "We are still gathering information on the fatal shooting of Judge Ramirez in the 312th District Court." They all froze at the announcement. The newswoman had one of those voices that didn't match her California, movie star looks.

She slightly leaned forward towards the camera as she reported the details of the shooting. If she was reading from a teleprompter, they couldn't tell. She may as well have been reading the ingredients in enchiladas. She told of the artery that had been nicked, and the copious amounts of blood that had been spilled on the steps. She reported that he had been making his way through the dwindling Anti/Pro-war crowd toward his car when he was shot down. The screen switched to the courthouse yellow crime tape circling the massive granite steps leading up to the huge doors. In the background of the crime scene, they could see one of the military pods and a number of the uniformed servicemen carrying sniper rifles. They both looked at Jessica, and all three were relieved she had left when she did. Jessica was shocked. She didn't know him well, but she had interviewed potential jury members in his court the week before.

They finished watching the news, then agreed to all meet back for lunch later that afternoon. Jude was going to call the funeral home and see when she could start back to work. She wanted something to redirect her thoughts. She missed preparing the bodies and was anxious to get back to it. They certainly didn't shoot anybody or blow anything up. Jackson had meetings, and Jessica was already craving a nap.

Chapter 5

The Bat Cave

Jude made chicken salad sandwiches on croissants and opened up a bag of potato chips. Jackson grabbed three bottles of water and a jar of pickles while Jessica got plates and napkins. They seemed to all be eating a lot lately, but nobody was complaining. They ate at the bar in the kitchen enjoying light conversation, Jessica eyeballing the fresh apple pie on the counter.

"Hey guys," said Jackson, "there's something important I want to talk to you about, but don't freak out." Jessica and Jude looked at him as if he'd grown a second head. "It's called a Safe Place. Dad and I built it, just in case we ever needed it. With the military moving into the bigger cities, things may start moving closer in toward the suburbs. We need to be prepared."

"I can't believe it has escalated this fast just since your Dad died," Jude said.

Jackson produced a yellow pencil and tablet. Everybody was quiet, all eyes on the tablet. Jessica slid the dishes to one side of the bar to make room and grabbed another water bottle instead of the dessert and coffee her mom offered.

"Wait a minute," Jessica said, "don't you have a phone app we can all look at? What's with the old school paper and pencil? Mom's house is solid antiques, but I know we all have upgraded cell phones." Jude and Jackson wordlessly looked up at her like she spoke in an unknown tongue and continued with the yellow #2 pencil.

"There may come a time that our cell phones don't work," said Jude, slipping on her reading glasses. "We're here to discuss a plan for when and if the worst comes."

"Oh. I didn't think about all of that. Okay. I understand. Whatever. Third world problems," she conceded.

Jackson took a deep breath. "Okay, guys, brace yourselves. You're going to be surprised, but that seems to be the theme this week," he said, glancing over at Jessica. "We need to be prepared if—when the attacks start here. We're surrounded by military bases, so it makes sense to assume we may very well be the first targets."

Jessica interrupted, "I knew it!" She said, "The last four years we weakened our military. Huge mistake. Now we look like a bunch of weak-assed—uhhh, sorry, Mom—wimpy, tree-hugging Americans!"

"Jessica," Jude scolded.

"I used a sentence enhancer. My bad," said Jessica, "but it makes me mad, and I can't help thinking that!"

"Jackson, finish what you were saying while I get a bar of soap in case Jessica has anymore outbursts," Jude teased. She and Jessica giggled.

"Guys, come on. This is serious."

"We know," Jude said. "We're just a little on edge. Our emotions are all over the board today."

Jackson nodded. He certainly agreed with that analogy. "Like I was trying to tell you, Dad and I bought a piece of property just outside of Decatur. It's about 1200 acres." He paused for effect. Their mouths both dropped open. "Yeah," he said. "Seriously, it's awesome, like the old bomb shelters they built in the 60's, but way bigger. It also has a complete underground bunker and tunnel system behind one of the dirt walls. Some of it's blocked in. This place is right out of a serial killer's dream."

Both the women sat and stared at him, speechless. Jude rubbed down the goosebumps on her arms. Jessica was the first to speak. "Dude, this is wild! Are you serious? You and Dad actually followed through with all that talk of underground forts and solar panels? Why didn't I see any paperwork on the deed or some loan documents? This is all getting weirder by the second. You're starting to freak me out."

"Well, we all *need* to be a little freaked out," he replied. "It just might keep us alive—maybe keep our heads attached to our shoulders. And the reason you didn't see the paperwork is because it's in my name for a tax write-off."

Jude nervously cut another piece of pie and put it on Jackson's plate while he carefully drew a map with lots of squiggles and landmarks.

"What all is out there? Is it livable? Can we eat and sleep there?" she asked.

Jackson glanced up at her face. That was his mom. She didn't cry out in hysteria or shrink back at the news of the possibility of going into underground hiding. Her first thought was how they would survive. He had always admired her courage to face whatever.

"Did you get any further than just purchasing it?" she continued, looking intently at him.

"It's way further, Mom," he mumbled, with a big bite of the pie in his mouth.

At this point, Jessica stood to her feet. "This is insane; this is crazy talk guys. Do you really think it's going to come to that? Like we're really going to have to move out to the woods? I was hoping the Rapture would happen before anything like this started. At least, that's how they always make it sound in church—like we're just going to float away while the rest of the world is blown to smithereens. I feel like I'm having an out-of-body experience here. Secret cellars. Hideouts." Jessica sat back down shaking her head. "I was hoping we could avoid this. I was hoping the Christians would be taken before America got tagged or blown off the map."

Jackson looked up and said, "Why in the world would we not expect America to suffer in some degree for her part in all of this?"

"This is very serious," said Jude. "I can feel it in my bones. Let's get our plan together."

Before they could wrap their minds around it all, they were in Jackson's black SUV heading up Highway 287 in total silence and anticipation. Jude, with her hair pulled into a quick ponytail, sat in the front seat wearing a pair of faded jeans and a long sleeved T. Jessica had thrown on sweats, while Jackson had full-on camouflage. They all had grabbed jackets and sunglasses on their way out of the front door. Jackson had strapped on a Sig .45 caliber pistol—not the kind made for target practice; the kind that would take an enemy down.

It wasn't freezing outside, but there was a definite chill in the frosty Texas air. They were a far cry from the "city slickers" who had just driven off from their Colleyville home. After about an hour, they turned down a paved road and drove for about 10 more miles.

"Wow," said Jessica, "I didn't know there was actual country this close to Fort Worth."

"Wait 'til you see it," Jackson replied. "It's really going to blow your hair back."

"Well, my hair's already blown back," said Jude, as she thought of the possibility of having to leave their home under the cloak of darkness. They all giggled at her remark and kept going.

Jackson's adrenalin was pumping 90 to nothing when he began to slow the vehicle down and eased off down the embankment onto a gravel road.

He maneuvered the bulky vehicle just around an outcropping of iron ore rocks and dingy white boulders and parked in the middle of them. It was like a hidden, off-road garage.

Jessica was the first to open her door. "I feel like I'm one of the freaky *Twilight Zone* people." She slammed her door and opened Jude's. "Come on, Mom. Welcome to *Deliverance*."

"Not funny," Jude replied, emphasizing the "f" with a stiff facial expression, feeling like she was about to be asked to walk the plank.

"Mom, it's going to be fine. Come on, follow me," Jackson said, taking her arm.

They walked about 30 feet into the woods, and then, as if he was counting his steps, he stopped and pulled back a huge entanglement of draping, evergreen vines. They all stepped through the "rabbit hole." There in front of them was a camouflage, off-road Jeep (the kind seen in old war pictures), partially hidden under a pine needle-covered tarp. Jackson pulled it off and tossed it to the side.

Jude instructed everyone to fasten their seatbelts, and away they went. They splashed through little creeks and valleys. Jude yelled loudly over the roar of the engine, "Is all of this land really ours?"

"All 1200 acres!" he yelled back. They went on for several more minutes up a steep embankment and over some rolling hills, somewhat gently bouncing and jostling around in the Jeep until they finally went into a dark cave of some sort. He cut the engine off, and they all sat silently for a moment in the pitch black. "Are you okay, Jessica? I tried to take it as easy as I could for you."

"Yeah, I'm good," she said. "Is this some kind of a bat cave? I would think this was cool if I was still about ten years old and didn't feel like I was running for my life."

Jackson clicked on a huge flashlight he had slipped over his head—miner's gear. "It's not creepy. I promise. I love it here. All those camping and hunting trips we took—this is where we came. Y'all come on, there's way more to see. Just watch your step."

They all snickered at his appearance with the big light strapped to his forehead. So out of character for him—for all of them. Sure, Jude loved her houseful of beautiful antiques, and the thought of another time period was enchanting, even romantic. She thought of big pots of stew cooking over an open fire while your man hunted game. She wasn't quite sure she could take a shoelace or a couple of sticks to actually build a fire or anything though.

They followed him several more feet through the damp cave. "This reminds me of a gold or silver mine back in the 1800's," Jude whispered nervously. "Glad I wore my boots. Yuck," she said, stepping through a soggy patch of muddy slush.

"It's okay, Mom, you don't have to whisper," said Jackson. "And you can't expect marble floors when you go into hiding out in the woods."

"Yeah," said Jessica, scraping three inches of something off of the sole of her shoe. "You wouldn't be able to keep them clean out here." They both glanced at each other and snickered. They knew their mom was a city girl and her idea of camping was in a $200,000 mountain cabin with picturesque views and a hot tub. Right now, she was on the lookout for bugs and bats.

He took them to the entrance. It was obscured by still more vines, but there it was—an old, slanted storm door with stairs leading down into the darkness. Jackson aimed the flashlight in and down they went. The door slammed abruptly behind them making them all jump. They stood quiet for a moment while their eyes adjusted. Then they heard a rustling, cracking sound. *Oh, my gosh! Was somebody hiding down here?* They all froze.

Jackson reached up and cut the headlamp off. "Nobody move," he whispered. Jude and Jessica were clutching hands, squinting in the darkness. Jackson's hands moved with cat-like reflexes: one signaling for total silence; the other moving to the pistol still holstered at his waist. He turned toward the sound, preparing to draw and fire at any moment. He could hear his heart pounding in his ears. Jude was straining into the darkness to try and see the ground in front of them. Jessica instinctively put her hand across her abdomen. They couldn't even hear her breathing. Jackson silently moved towards the sound. *"It'll be a showdown for sure. I didn't bring my mother and pregnant sister out here for this! You don't come on our land uninvited,"* he thought to himself.

This was Texas. He would protect them at any cost. Out of the darkness, two glassy eyes met his. He clicked on the headlight quickly. There it was! Hissing, clawing and scratching and looking for a quick way out. Jackson jumped about a foot back onto the girls. Jude screamed as he grazed across her foot!

"What is that?" she shrieked (nearly crawling up his back).

"It's a possum!" he said, still backing up with the headlamp knocked askew covering one eye like a pirate.

"You could have fooled me!" yelled Jessica, as she jumped back in a thwarted effort to climb the wall. They continued screaming and tripping over one another as they gave the possum a wide birth to make its escape. He scurried past them and darted out through a ratty part of the shelter door. After their hearts finally stopped racing and they had all gained their composures from the near-death experience, they headed deeper into the cave and into a long hall, exercising a little more caution.

There were several torches, wax candles and lanterns hanging everywhere with a slight smell of lamp oil in the hall, but other than that, the air was normal. They made their way a few more feet deeper into the cave. All the floors had gone from dirt to rustic hardwoods once they left the initial cellar area.

Jackson gave them each a lamp and clicked off the headlight but kept it fastened on. It had begun to feel a little claustrophobic with the cave, the darkness, the headpiece squeezing in on the sides of his head. But there was a lot to show them, so he continued giving them the guided tour. There was a great room with rustic style couches and heavy wooden tables. It had a huge kitchen area with two long eating tables that could easily seat 10 to 15 people each. There was a semi-crude cooking area with a copper pan holder suspended from the ceiling, holding pots hanging on individual hooks. There were containers of dry goods including pounds of beans and rice products all stored in waterproof, animal-proof containers. Possums couldn't get into this part of the cave, but they wanted to play it safe. There were pipes snaking their way up to the ground above for ventilation and a septic system to accommodate the bathrooms. There were a few private sleeping chambers as well as a community room full of bunks like you'd see at youth camp.

"What was this place?" asked Jude.

"Dad said it was old underground escape tunnels during the slavery days. Then the previous owners had sort of upgraded parts of it and some of the tunnels leading out had been closed off completely to control unwelcome intruders." They finished seeing everything and headed back out.

"Well," said Jude, checking her hair for spiderwebs, "we could certainly make do with these accommodations if we had to." They all agreed it was indeed the perfect hiding place.

Chapter 6

Dr. Feel Good

Jude stepped out of the tunnels, grateful to get back into the bright sunlight. She paused for a moment to feel the expanse of the open space, the bulk of the massive oak trees, the musky scent of freshly fallen pine needles. She lingered for just a moment, taking it all in. She gazed up into the heavens, admiring His magnificent handiwork. The mounds of gorgeous white clouds peeked through lofty pines, and sunrays cascaded through the leaves. She took it all in, but no longer for granted. She silently thanked God for her family and vowed to continue to trust in Him alone.

On the ride back home, they discussed where to meet and what to do in case of a catastrophic event or anything they felt would jeopardize their safety. Like Jude had reminded them earlier, there might not be cell phone reception during such a time. They would each do their best to get to the hideout and each one leave a clue at her house to let the others know. After careful consideration, they decided on a refrigerator note with no writing, just a Post-it held by a magnetized clip. She kept all of her note pads and postage paraphernalia in a small utility drawer next to the fridge. They were all familiar with it; they had dug around in it for years. Each one chose a different color. The color would indicate who had left.

It had been years since Jude's refrigerator had displayed the fine artwork of her children. For years, each prized piece had been dutifully held up with magnets. Some were vacation magnets from their trip to the Grand Canyon and Hollywood; others were from Carlsbad Caverns and the crystallite they had mined there. But most of them were magnetized advertisements like pizza and Chinese delivery services that had come in the mail. It was hard for Jude to throw away a magnet.

As they continued to make their way back home, they noticed a station of sorts below the new mixmaster at I-35 and 820. Nothing big. Just a subtle presence of military close to the Lake Worth base. They could see the base but really couldn't make out any details this late in the evening. They could, however, hear the military helicopters flying back to the base. They could see twenty five or so as they craned their necks to get a better look. They rode the rest of the way in silence, exited off on Hwy 26, and before long, they were home. The house loomed large and dark as they pulled up into the driveway. Jackson dropped them off and headed to the gym.

Jude unlocked the front door and turned on the light in the foyer. "I'll put on some tea, Mom. Orange or chamomile?"

"Definitely the chamomile," said Jude, pulling the elastic band out of her hair. "Honestly, I need the comfort."

"Should we get showers first? Or just wait?" asked Jessica.

"Gosh, that sounds great," Jude replied. "Let's get our showers first so we can relax."

They were freshly showered, both in black yoga pants and white T-shirts. The ladies at the Country Club would probably have asked her to resign if they knew she was wearing white T's from the local department store every evening. Jude had loved the feel of a T-shirt since she was just a little girl. She had often said they reminded her of her sweet daddy. He had worn one every day of his life—not the V necks; they had to be round. Her daddy and mother had gone home to be with the Lord nearly a decade ago. She still missed them and thought about them every day, and with the world in such chaos, she felt like it wouldn't be long until they were all together again.

The kettle was whistling in just moments, and Jessica brought them both a cup of hot tea served in her grandmother's china. They were eggshell white with blue hand-painted morning glories carefully displayed on each one. Jude looked up at her in surprise. "In Mimi's good china?"

"Why not?" said Jessica, shrugging her shoulders. "According to Jackson, we may not have long to drink anything besides well water out in the country." They both met each other's eyes in a cross between humor and sarcasm.

"Well, bottoms up," said Jude, with a smile on her face. And they held their cups up to toast Mimi and Papa in heaven.

They cozied up on the deep, cushiony sofa, settling in to sip the hot tea. Jude smiled as she smelled the dollop of honey melting at the bottom of her cup. She was reminded of when the kids were young and how they would hold the empty cup up trying to get that last drop of the sweet goodness.

The den, with its low lighting in the evenings, was the perfect place to finish out the days. Mostly beiges with a few splashes of sage green. It was very, very inviting. They sat on opposite ends of the couch and curled their feet up. No mention of babies or hideouts. Jude leaned over and grabbed a throw out of a large wicker basket and then clicked on the TV. They both listened as the local newsman gave his interpretation of current events.

"Many high profile preachers and evangelicals are whispering words like martial law, government takeover, End Times, the Rapture and Armageddon," exclaimed the newsman. He was about 35 with Harvard charm and immovable, plastic-like hair—the kind of hair gale force winds couldn't move. "What we do know is there is war raging all around us. Russia and China have both pulled out of the UN, parts of South America, including Mexico, are burning. The possibilities are terrifying. We have hundreds of troops deployed. Our warships are out in the Gulf and the open seas. Huge battleships in full force are standing at the ready. We have a special guest tonight, a world-renowned evangelist, and he is going to give us his take on the global pulse; hopefully, a detailed clip on how it all relates to Bible prophecy. Many Christians believe we are standing in the doorway, the very threshold of what Believers are calling the great Tribulation. The plans for the Temple in Jerusalem have been revealed today and the 'Church' has confirmed that they are indeed referred to in the Bible. All the implements needed to begin sacrifices and temple requirements are all 'a go.' There's talk of red heifers and the possible discovery of the Ark of the Covenant."

Jude and Jessica both turned to stare at each other in disbelief. The newsman introduced the guest speaker, whom some of the stoics refer to as Brother "Feel Good." He was always grinning and had kind eyes, commanding his audiences with his very presence. He faced the camera and began to speak as the newsroom erupted in applause. "The Bible tells us of End Times where we will know the season. No man knows the hour or the day, not even Jesus Himself, but the Father ... the Father knows. The Scriptures instruct us to watch," he said, in his heavy, southern drawl. "In light of the recent events of Russia and China, I would definitely say we are standing in the doorway of the end of the world as we know it."

A hush fell over the newsroom as well as every household in America watching. "The Rapture could happen any day. The Second Coming and the Rapture are two separate events," he explained. "There are prophecies that have to be fulfilled to usher in the Second Coming, but not the Rapture. We are living in the days of Pentecost, or the 'Harvest,' if you please. For those who understand the correlation that the seven Jewish feasts have on everything, the next sound the Saved will hear? The blast of the trumpet! Are you ready? I encourage you to open your Bibles and dig deep before it's too late. Go to your local churches, tune in to the many television stations teaching on the Last Days. Or call the (800) number at the bottom of your TV screen if you have questions or need prayer. Most of all, America, watch, your Redeemer draws nigh!"

All at once, the TV scrambled. Then nothing. The screen went completely black. Jude's hair stood up on its ends. That couldn't have been a coincidence, not this time.

Chapter 7

The Census

It had been many weeks since they had gone to Decatur to see the hideout and had listened to the guest speaker on world news and biblical prophecies. Winter had completely settled in as Thanksgiving and Christmas had quietly come and gone with a small turkey and a handful of gifts. February had brought the typical Texas ice storms, but thankfully, they were short-lived.

The world had groaned and travailed through more metamorphoses in the nearly five months since Grayson had died. Jude thought it seemed like another lifetime ago. There had been such an anti-Christian uproar over the news broadcast regarding the Tribulation that the local authorities had been on high alert and patrolling every suburb and housing district. The anti-Christian mobs had burned crosses and churches and people were persecuted for even wearing a cross necklace.

A census had been sent to each home requesting "friendly" information. Basics: How many occupants in the home, place of employment, religious preference. People had just blindly filled them out, going along like sheep, doing what they were told. They had moved past the unobtrusive mailings and had begun knocking on doors to get the information. Jessica had filled out the census claiming dual residency. Jackson, since nobody was aware of the flat, kept his name off any lists. They suspected there might come a time when running under the radar might become necessary.

The USA had engaged nationwide as attacks came out of nowhere. Even the shores of Florida and California had been bombed, along with New York and Galveston Bay with sleeper cells that evaded Homeland Security. ISIS had reared its ugly head in a handful of states, murdering Christians and blowing up what they could before being captured and executed. The media showed it all: the decapitations, burning bodies alive. They claimed it was the only way Americans in the rural areas would be convinced they were in wartime. Nobody trusted the media. Farmers weren't as close to the war as the citizens of the capitals and inner cities. Some didn't realize the depth of what was going on around them. They just continued to bale hay and milk their cows, refusing to believe it had all come to this.

In world news, China had unveiled one of five aircraft carriers in their waters, non-verbally letting the world know they were for China. Period. Russia, though not disclosing or confirming, had obviously fortified Iran with nuclear weapons, billions of dollars in bombs, ground power and obviously prepared to step in whenever and with whomever they chose. Since America had officially declared War, they had finally sent at least a handful of troops to aid with the defense of that sacred patch of the long fought-over land called The Holy Land—Israel. The world was holding its breath waiting for Iran to stop pelting and start bombing.

People were starting to panic. The murder rate had more than doubled in the inner cities. The lower income suburb residents and whack jobs had all come out of the woodwork to riot and loot. Congress had expedited a temporary martial law bill to help control the states, and it was immediately signed off on by the President. A curfew was established in every city and suburb. Streets cleared by 10:00 p.m. or people would be arrested and spend the night in jail. The criminals were not allowed to take control of the cities because they were angry—not here in Texas. They were hauled off to jail or gassed until they went back home, waiting for the next day, and then they would start all over again. It was clear to Jude and her family things were on the brink of becoming unmanageable when society began to unravel.

Jackson said they were being watched at every turn. Even the red dot that comes on the laptop, supposedly just for a camera, had been utilized to "communicate with the public for a test" they had called it. They had come across every computer that was on the Internet like the loud obnoxious beep that interrupts a favorite program declaring "a test of the network should there be a real emergency." Jude was horrified that while soaking in the tub watching her favorite flix, she may have been watched. She was furious with the invasion of privacy and had told Jackson she sure hoped the government had approved of her brand of bath salts!

Chapter 8

The Funeral Home

Life, as the Mitlows had known it for decades, was over. Along with the rest of the world, they had moved on as best as they could with this different life. Jackson was hardly ever at the gym and had so far eluded the census people. Jessica was mostly at her mother's and worked out of the house when she could.

At 19 weeks, she was beginning to show her baby bump. Mercifully, the nausea had passed. The last sonogram had revealed the gender—a baby boy. Still no luck reaching Tony, although his Division had assured her they were making every attempt to find him.

Bodies were coming in by the droves to the funeral home. Jude went back to work. She was more than ready; and she wanted to help. With all the violent protests and the overseas soldiers being sent home in black body bags, they needed her.

Jude had come in early this morning. She was mentally sorting through the bodies. There were nine soldiers, four grandmas who had all succumbed to heart failure, one grandpa who had a 1:00 p.m. service and a six-month-old fetus—pre-term delivery. First, she would get grandpa ready to move to the Chapel, then dress the soldiers while the curling irons were heating for the grandmothers' hair. Lastly, she would take care of the tiny infant.

One of the funeral directors poked his head in the prep room on his way to the Chapel, carrying an armload of red gladiolas (or funeral flowers as her mother had always referred to them). They were gorgeous. He asked if she could meet with Daniel Wayne, the General Manager/Owner, in his office before she left for the day.

Jude looked up from the curling iron in grandma number four's hair, peering over her reading glasses. She nodded and shrugged her shoulders. "Yeah, sure," she replied. "I'll be finished up around 4:00." Jude thought it was unusual for him to ask to see her. She had been in and out of the funeral home for years and had never met him. *"Hmmmmm,"* she thought, *"maybe I'm about to be let go. Whatever."*

He worked on the other side of the building from the prep room. She would come in the back door and discreetly leave the same way. She rarely saw any of the employees except the embalmers who stayed tucked away in the prep room throughout the years.

She had heard typical office puffed-up tales about Mr. Wayne—war stories. He was a retired serviceman, Medic/Special Ops. Gossip in the prep room included words and rhetoric like special agent, hero, having the ability to deliver a baby—apparently in mid-air while hanging off the back of an Army tank, no less, in the desert. Jude chuckled to herself at the stories. A part of her wanted to meet this guy, see what all the uproar was about or if he could really walk on water and leap buildings in a single bound.

It was nearly four o'clock. Jude was tired but felt accomplished. She wrapped the tiny infant in the pink blanket the family had provided and brushed on some "youthful glow" to the pale, bloodless lips to restore that baby pink look. She gently laid the tiny, little girl in the white miniature casket and went to the sink to scrub out. She always thought the little caskets were so despondent, with or without a child in them. To her, they represented premature loss, grieving mothers, heartbroken dads. It relieved her to know Jessica's pregnancy was progressing as normal. Dismissing that thought for now, she hung up her lab coat and stopped by the restroom.

Hurrying, she pulled her hair out of the matronly bun and quickly reapplied lipstick and freshened up her perfume before going in to see Mr. Wayne. She fanned her hands wildly so as not to arrive in a big cloud of spicy musk. The only contact she had ever had with him was a sympathy card attached to a huge peace lily she had received the week after Grayson had passed. Unusual as it was for him to request to see her, she didn't want to go in smelling like formaldehyde and cheap mega-hold hairspray. Even if she was about to be fired, she wanted to look good. Why else would he be summoning her except to terminate her?

The funeral home receptionist, Lucy, dutifully guided Jude through the dimly lit hallways to reach Mr. Wayne's office. Funeral homes were so quiet and dark with very few rays of light reaching into their depths. Not everybody could work in that atmosphere Jude knew, but the rest of her co-workers felt as much at home there as they did anywhere. After a couple of twists and turns by the sample markers and at the Chapel doors, they arrived at his office. Lucy knocked lightly and was greeted by a strong voice on the other side.

Daniel Wayne had been in and out of this funeral home since he was in high school. Every nook and cranny, every office, every coat of paint, he had been a witness to over the course of the last 30 years. It's where he had met his beautiful wife when they were just seniors. Her family owned it, actually (a detail she "forgot" to mention for quite some time).

Her name was Margaret Ann Ransom—Maggi for short. They had both worked in the cool dark halls of the funeral home for an entire summer before she ever told him it was her father who owned it. Her father was hoping she would take over the family business, but nothing doing—Maggi had her own ideas. She, like Daniel, had her sights set on the Army. They both dreamed of being Army medics, and that's exactly what they did. Soon after graduation, they married and went off to boot camp, much to their families' chagrin.

The Army discovered Daniel's uncanny ability to learn foreign languages quickly and trained him to be a medic/interpreter over the next few years. It came in handy during Desert Storm as he could get into many places others couldn't under the façade of medical supplies being delivered and his ability to speak perfect Arabic.

Maggi had done her tours on the buddy system with him for many years until she discovered she was pregnant. She nearly gave the whole platoon's location away during a bout of morning sickness. By that evening, she was on a jet headed to Germany and from there, stateside. After their son, Spencer Ransom Wayne, was born, she had a three-month maternity leave of absence. She was already nearing the end of her tour of duty, and they both agreed she should stay home and care for the baby and fulfill her father's lifelong dream of her working in the family business.

She got her mortuary licenses and actually developed an immediate love for taking care of the funeral home business. Spencer grew up in the Chapel and casket showcases at Eternal Rest Funeral Home.

Daniel loved the Army and stayed in long enough to retire with many honors, stripes and two purple hearts. Not long after he returned home, Maggi's parents both tragically died in Tower One on 9/11 while vacationing in New York City. Daniel had stepped right up and was the perfect shoo-in for the funeral home. He went through a two-year program and became fully licensed, and they were once again happily working together.

They received the news just before Christmas, the year Spencer turned 17, through a routine breast exam and mammography, that Maggi had Stage III breast cancer. She did the radical surgeries and all of the chemo and radiation her body could handle, but after an 18-month battle, she died in the hospital on a warm, summer morning. They both took it hard, but together they came out of the storm of grief and finally made peace with it all.

Daniel casually contemplated dating after about five years, but mostly he just threw himself into his work. One of the funeral home directors he had lunch with occasionally told him about the contract hairdresser who worked in the prep room. He hadn't gone out of his way to go down there and meet her, but wasn't opposed to it either. As a rule, he didn't have a lot of personal interaction with co-workers beyond holiday lunches and a yearly review. He had nothing against any of them—actually cared about all of them—but still had a slight wall around himself, not visible to many. But now ... on the other side of the door was the woman he had heard a lot about lately.

Daniel came from behind the heavy oak desk with his hand out. He was tall, sharp and had piercing eyes the color of chestnuts. He was good-looking, around 50, with mostly dark hair that had a dash of silver. His high gloss shoes were the same coal black as the suit he wore. She probably couldn't have found a speck of lint on his coat with a search warrant. He was definitely military. She hoped her pants weren't wrinkled or had any loose strands of grandma's silver hair on them. He had a firm handshake. It was his eyes that first captured and held her attention. There was something about them—almost identical to Grayson's.

"Please, sit. Can I get you anything?" he asked. "Water, soda, coffee?"

"Coffee would be great," she replied, and sat down in the proffered chair, thanking the sweet angels of mercy she had stopped by the restroom and taken that bun down. At least she had dressed in her "nice funeral clothes." Today, she had worn black slacks with a pale pink sweater and matching pumps. Although she wore a lab coat and gloves over her clothes for prep, she was always prepared to meet with a family if called upon to do so. She felt she was fairly comfortable with him already. She was grinning like a school girl. *"Really?"* she scolded herself, *"are you fifteen?"* From what she could tell, all the rumors were true. No exaggeration here. Funeral home people are of a kindred spirit. They feel like they've known each other forever after only about 15 minutes.

"Well," thought Daniel, *"I need to get down to the other end of the building a little more often. Exactly what are you grinning at? Get ahold of yourself there, Captain,"* he admonished himself, *"before you make a fool of yourself."*

He sent Lucy for the coffee and extended his condolences once again for the untimely death of her husband. "What has it been now, a few months?" he inquired, never taking his eyes from hers.

"Several," said Jude. "I've had to adapt quickly. It feels more like years." He was nodding as she spoke. "Like I've told a thousand families, 'You miss them dearly, but time marches on.'"

Her mouth was suddenly devoid of any moisture—bone dry like cotton. *"Am I rambling?"* she asked herself nervously. *"I hope I haven't said anything stupid!"*

He watched her speak and enjoyed the sound of her voice. He couldn't help but notice those beautiful green eyes and the way she nervously kept stopping to catch her breath. *"She must be thirsty,"* he thought. "Where in the world is Lucy with that coffee?" he said out loud. "Grinding her own beans?" On cue, Lucy appeared at the door. Lucy was short, plump, chesty. She donned a tall stack of white hair. She was one of those women who looked like she had been 65 her whole life. Jude thought it was like looking at her mother's old 1950's school annuals. You couldn't tell the students from the teachers. Lucy was strictly business and very observant. She knew everything that went on in the funeral home. And kindly put, Jude had heard she was the "go-to person" and seemed to like it that way.

"Well, I'm sure you must be curious as to why I wanted to see you today," Daniel said, as he sat down behind the desk. "First, I wanted to tell you how much we have appreciated and admired your service to our funeral home."

"Well, here it comes," she thought to herself, *"termination, sandwiched between two compliments."* She unconsciously sat up a little straighter and crossed her legs.

"It's been brought to my attention—well, you know, I don't get down to that end of the building often—that you've done a great job for us. It's in the details that people remember a funeral. I wanted to tell you that your 'details' have been much appreciated and duly noted." *"Did I seriously just say 'duly noted'?"* He replayed the sentence in his mind. *"Wow, clever. Hope this isn't my new A-game,"* he said to himself.

"He is all male," she mused. *"Strong, built like a general. Broad shoulders, narrow waist—seriously?"* she admonished herself once again. *"What the heck are you thinking?"* She hoped he couldn't read her mind. She barely could. She may have been called in there to be fired, but she had certainly given Mr. Wayne a thorough examination. She could now feel the blood rushing to her face. *"This is ridiculous. Only one other man has ever had this effect on me,"* she thought, *"and I spent the last 31 years as his wife."*

Chapter 9

I Spy Chemistry

The coffee smelled wonderful, maybe French roasted beans. She noticed the coffee service was from a pretty matching set, unlike the hodge-podge, colorful collection of cups in the breakroom sitting in a dishrack. They were from every local vendor in the area—cups from the office supply store; one from the casket supply company. They even had some from the florists.

She took the pretty white cup full of coffee and heavily creamed and sugared it. Thoughts of Grayson slipped through her mind for a split second. He always teased her about having coffee with her cream. She quickly laid that memory aside as she noticed Daniel had left his coffee jet black—not even one grain of sugar. He still hadn't taken his eyes off of her since she had arrived. She was still patiently waiting for the proverbial axe to drop. *"Let's just get to the point of the meeting,"* she thought, feeling suddenly warm. *"It must be 90° in this office. This is bound to be the world's most ill-timed hot flash of the ages, what with me feeling 15 years old again and everything."* She could feel herself beginning to perspire. She hoped to sweet Moses that her face wasn't turning blood red.

"Well," Mr. Wayne said, breaking the shrill noise of the clinking spoon in her cup. "The reason I wanted to talk to you—hrrrmp. That will be all, Lucy," Daniel said, clearing his throat as they both glanced over at her still standing in the doorway holding the empty tray.

Jude didn't want an audience for this. She wanted her to leave the room already, but all of a sudden, Jude noticed something familiar about her name tag. Her last name was Gargentella! *"How odd. That was Tony's last name—Jessica's Tony. Could it be a coincidence?"* she wondered.

"Sorry about that," he said, shaking his head and smiling, showing a perfect row of pearly whites. "She likes to keep up with all the 'current affairs.'" Ordinarily, Jude would have smiled or chuckled at the remark, but she didn't. She was still processing the whole last name thing, wondering what in the world. Tony said he had no living relatives.

"Oh, gosh. Was Daniel talking?" she thought. *"Oops."* She was so caught up in the Lucy name thing.

"But seriously," he continued, "with all the extra bodies we have coming in, I wanted to make sure you were able to keep up with the workload. I know you normally average 10 to 12 families a month, according to your invoices." He gestured with his hands as he flipped through a stack of papers. "That's just about doubled now, hasn't it? That's a lot of work, even with your experience. Do you need more help?"

Jude quickly answered, trying to stay focused. "Honestly, I haven't really had the chance to think about it."

"Well," said Daniel. I may have a solution to that problem. I've seriously thought about getting back in the physical aspect of the operations myself." As he realized what he had just said, he thought, *"I what? I want to help in the prep room? That's news to me. I haven't even considered that notion in years! Why did I just say that?!"*

"I've lost several employees due to all of the attacks. People are all about home and hearth right now. Some have even rejoined their families in other states. I don't blame them, but it has left us a little shorthanded. What I'd like to know is, what can I do to help you?" he said, leaning back in his chair.

"I don't know. I've been so busy I haven't thought about it," she said joyfully, realizing she wasn't there to be let go. She didn't need the money; she was comfortable in that regard, but she loved her work, and now, she had another interest in coming to the funeral home. "I actually don't mind the extra work. It gives me purpose, and it gets me away from the television with all the terrible stories of war and death. It's nice to steal away and think of something else for a few hours. My son just remarked yesterday that we could wake up one morning with the whole town bombed or overrun with soldiers. Even the earthquakes seem to be getting closer."

"I know what you mean," agreed Daniel, shaking his head. "It's still so unreal. The funeral home is the only thing that keeps me and my son grounded these days."

"Oh, you have a son, too? That's awesome," Jude said. "How old is your boy?" she asked. Both of them were enjoying the mutual conversation, momentarily forgetting his original question of help in the prep room.

Daniel was intrigued with her and already knew he wanted to know everything there was to know about Jude Mitlow. "He's 27," he replied, "and he's really great."

"That's so wonderful," Jude said, smiling. "And back to your original question, I really do need help with the bodies. With the amount coming in, and especially the heavier ones, I can always use help. Even with the remote controlled lift," she said, leaning over and placing her hand on his desk, "I still have to get the straps underneath them. And I really would enjoy the company," she added. *"Wow,"* she thought, *"I'm not wasting any time, am I?"*

"Perfect," said Daniel, as he picked up the phone and hit '0.' "Lucy, send Spencer in, please."

While they were waiting for Spencer, Jude glanced out the window and noticed a redbird sitting on the budding branch of a small oak tree. She loved the beginning of spring; everything begins to come to life again with new possibilities. The beautiful grounds of the funeral home were maintained immaculately. The cardinal flew over to the top of a nearby juniper. The bright red of the cardinal against the contrast of the dark, green foliage was absolutely breathtaking.

Her mind wondered momentarily, thinking of home and Jessica, the baby and Jackson. She snapped out of it when a tall, younger, good-looking guy walked into the room. He was sharply dressed in a dark suit and a crisp white shirt. He had close-cropped dark hair with the same build and same piercing eyes as Daniel. She could tell at once they were related by the way they both carried themselves and their impeccable appearance.

"Jude, this is my son, Spencer," Daniel said, standing up and walking around to the front of the desk to introduce them. "He's taking a couple of semesters off from the University to help me out here in the funeral home. With everything that's going on around us, we decided for now the education would go on hold."

Spencer nodded in agreement, glancing back and forth from Daniel to Jude.

"Hi, Spencer." She stood and held out her hand and smiled at him. "Do you go by Spence or the whole thing?"

"Either way is fine," he replied, shaking her hand and giving her a semi-smile.

"Yes, the same eyes," Jude thought to herself.

"My dad calls me Spencer, but I answer to both."

He was warm and friendly, just like his father, and he had that same air about him. She just knew, he, too, had above average intelligence. They all stood there for a minute. Everything got quiet for just a tad too long. Daniel and Spencer both looked at each other and grinned.

"Well, what's up, Dad? Should we sit?" Spencer pressed with an open palm sweeping to Jude's chair. Jude suspected he was trying to move along the conversation. "What's on your mind, Dad?" They were all three still just standing there.

Daniel shook off his fog and said, "Yes, yes, let's sit." They both waited for Jude to take her seat, and then Daniel went back behind his desk as Spencer sat in the chair next to Jude's. They both crossed their legs simultaneously. Jude glanced over at him and smiled.

"Okay," Daniel said, "Jude needs some help in the prep room. Think you could give us a hand?"

"Us?" Spencer said, surprised, as he made rapid back and forth hand gestures between he and Daniel. "You're going to help, too?"

Spencer found that very odd. His dad hadn't been in the prep room more than a dozen times in the last several years.

"Well, that is my name on the door last time I checked. I want to roll my sleeves up and get back into action where I'm needed," he said, as he clasped his hands together making a popping noise. "It's going to take all of us."

"Uhhhhh, okay," Spencer said, deciding he'd play along as he glanced over at Daniel's clasped hands. Another long, pregnant pause ensued. "Well, all right then," Spencer said, trying to close the conversation. Obviously his dad was having trouble putting two words together.

"Perfect," said Daniel, "that settles it then. We'll meet you back there around 10:00 in the morning."

"Sounds great," Jude said, feeling pleased with the new arrangements.

"Works for me," agreed Spencer, looking at his dad and then back at Jude.

"Well, if that's all," she said, standing to her feet, "I guess I'll see you guys tomorrow." Both of them stood up, and Daniel once again walked back from around the big desk.

"Good to meet you," said Spencer.

"It was good to meet you, too," said Jude, looking up at him.

"May I show you out?" said Daniel, immediately feeling dumb for asking. He wasn't on a date; he was talking to an employee.

"Oh, uhhh, that's not necessary," replied Jude, pulling her hair all toward the front of one shoulder and holding it while she talked. "I know my way around here pretty good. I'm sure you guys have more important things to do. I'm headed to my house anyway."

Jude walked to the door and opened it. "Well, it's been great meeting you and visiting with you," she said. "I, for one, am looking forward to all of us working together."

"We'll see you tomorrow, then," said Daniel. "Oh, and thanks for all your hard work," he stammered. Spencer was getting a kick out of it. He wasn't used to his dad tripping over any words or action. He was always well rehearsed in everything he tackled; always ready with a quick reply.

Today, in front of this woman, he was floundering, and he just kept that pace up. "It really means a lot. Your work, I mean. It's ... it's a gift." Spencer painfully watched on.

Jude blushed again at the compliment. She was ready to go to the car. "Well, thank you, sir—uhhh, Mr. Wayne."

"Please," he said abruptly, holding both hands up in protest, "call me Daniel." Jude immediately averted her eyes to the floor.

"Well, okay, Daniel," she said, slightly uncomfortable trying out the new name with Spencer looking on. "Daniel it is then." She glanced up at him and smiled one more time and quickly hurried down the hall.

Daniel and Spencer exchanged glances after she turned the corner in the direction of the prep room.

"What was that, Dad?" Spencer inquired.

"What was what?" Daniel said, nonchalantly.

"Dude, didn't her husband just die?"

"Yeah, several months ago—dude."

Spencer playfully mocked him. "You mean like two?"

"No, longer than that, more like five," Daniel corrected him. They briefly looked at each other, and Spencer turned and headed back to his own office, shaking his head. He hadn't seen his dad show this much interest in "the prep room" in years.

"Okay, that was awkward," he mumbled under his breath. "This ought to be interesting."

Jude stepped out of the office and into the warm, peaceful rays of the evening sun. She loved sunsets as much as she loved daybreak. She admired the beautiful palate of colors it displayed as if it had been painted from an artist's hand-held easel. Even with the distant roar of the flock of helicopters churning their way back to the base, it was still a nice evening. She, like the rest of the world, was becoming accustomed to all the military presence that was on every street corner, including the cemetery. Jude pushed the start button in her black, midsized car and shifted it into gear, and before she knew it, she was pulling into the garage. She guessed her mind had wandered during the fifteen-minute drive. (She didn't text and drive, but she had earned the gold for daydreaming and driving today.) Her thoughts were on Daniel, his son Spencer, and the new prep room arrangements. She replayed the whole day, calculating different sentences and phrases, remembering the looks and the conversation in general. It felt a little confusing, still not a year out from Grayson's tragic demise, but she had felt an attraction, and she knew Daniel had felt it, too.

Chapter 10

The Neighbors

She pressed the electronic door opener and pulled straight into the garage. While she was driving in, something caught her eye. Her neighbors had company. She had noticed them there before. In fact, she had noticed similar sightings all over the city. Tonight, they were here. Official-looking government cars parked next door. Several men dressed in black suits were looking her way while the neighbors slightly pointed and talked. They were standing in a tight little circle.

"What in the world?" Jude mumbled aloud as she got out of the car and started down the drive. She couldn't help but wonder exactly who they were. It just didn't sit well. She was heading down to the mailbox, still in her heels, when the neighbors and the Black Suits all lowered their voices and turned so as to not face her, speaking in hushed tones. Jude found this very strange—very unnerving. The closer she got to her brick mailbox, she began to sense something unfamiliar in the air. It felt dark, black, a heavy presence.

She saw something flash in one of their upstairs windows. Something was off here. She didn't know them like she did the rest of the people on her street. They had only moved in a few months ago. She fixed her eyes on the mailbox wishing she hadn't come to check it. In unison, they all turned to stare as she felt the hair stand up on her arms.

She stuck her hand into the deep box, half expecting something to grab her hand and pull her through into some sort of rabbit hole! She grabbed the stack of envelopes and hurried back into the garage, trying to escape their prying eyes as quickly as possible. In her rush, she caught one of her heels on the threshold of the garage, jerking one of her shoes off. She just kept going. She hit the electronic button and watched until the door closed all the way. The shoe had made the cut; it was in the

53

garage. She just left it there. She went in the house, pressed her back against the locked door and tried to catch her breath. She was glad it didn't require a key because her hands were shaking like a leaf. It would have been like a scene straight out of a horror movie when a screaming girl is trying to flee a crazed axe murderer, barely making it into the car, murderer hot on her heels, and she can't get the stupid key in the hole!

The garage door led through the laundry room and into the kitchen. She took a deep breath, calming herself. She could see the lights were on. "I'm setting the alarm," she shouted out, her heart still racing. "We're in for the evening."

She didn't have to look to know it was Jackson sitting at the kitchen bar on his laptop; she caught a glimpse of his neon green tank top. She thanked God he was there. She still had the hair standing up on her arms. "What's going on next door?" she asked breathlessly, as she walked right past him, tossing the mail on the bar. She was grateful he had moved back in with her. She headed straight into the living room to peek out of the window.

"I don't know," he said. "I haven't seen or heard anything unusual. What's the matter with you? Did something happen with that guy next door? Please tell me it did. I'd like half a chance to put him on the ground." He got up and followed her to the window, and they both peered out through the wooden slats of the shutters like spies, Jackson standing directly behind her, hovering.

"I can't put my finger on it," she whispered. "They didn't *DO* anything to me. It's just, well, there's something not right over there with those Suit guys there again. I could swear I saw a flash of something in that window upstairs."

"Seriously? Wonder what flashed?" he whispered back. "That has my creep meter going off. And those Suit guys are all over town."

Jude reached up and felt the back of her head. "Move over a little bit," she whispered. "I can feel your hot breath in my hair." He moved over to one side, and they both stood silently peering out at the strange neighbors and the Black Suit men as they appeared to be disbanding. "Who do you suppose those guys are?" asked Jude. "It felt like the devil himself."

"I have no idea," Jackson said, "but they don't know I'm here, and I don't plan to make it public knowledge. I've never liked that guy anyway. He's got better sense than to say anything to me or you. Ever since I backed Dad's Bimmer out of the drive and got a little too close to his St. Augustine, he's been a real jerk!"

"Oh, good grief," Jude whispered louder, feeling a little more at ease with the Suits driving off. "He's nearly let that grass burn up; they never water."

Jackson stared after her as she turned to walk out of the living room in a huff, satisfied that the Suits were leaving next door. *"Always the mother lion,"* he thought. He held up cat claws behind her as he followed her back into the kitchen, and they continued to discuss the Black Suits for a bit. Jude went upstairs to grab a quick shower and came back down fifteen minutes later. She had on her comfy yogas and T-shirt and made them both an omelet and a quick salad. They took their plates to the den and clicked on the TV. The new President was about to address the nation. Every living room in America was tuned in!

"The relentless missile and gun battles have gone on nonstop for hours in Syria, as well as Egypt, Iran and Iraq. It looks strangely like a distorted view of Las Vegas under siege with the cities lit up night and day," cried the newsman as they caught the tail end of the Channel 5 broadcast with Trent and Troy. Trent's voice was deep and authoritative as he spoke. He had the perfect "newsman voice." "Iran is a ticking time bomb," he said. "They have their thumb on the red button. It's just a matter of time before this thing goes nuclear, folks. Troy?" he said, turning his chair to the other anchorman.

Troy nodded. "Closer to home," he said, in an equally impressive voice as the camera zoomed in for a close-up, "more violent protests have broken out nationwide in the months subsequent to the election of our new President. We are waiting to hear from him right now as he determines the steps needed to try and bring this country into some kind of order." He stacked his papers and waited for Camera 3 to fade out.

Jude and Jackson listened intently as the screen shot switched from their local station to the Washington room reserved for speeches and press conferences. Red, white and blue; the stars and stripes. It was all so comforting to see the familiar podium and flags instead of just the burning cities and death. All America tuned in to hear the newly elected President, Fredrick Harrison, lay out his new plan of action to strengthen our military and defend our nation while urging all Americans to prepare for the worst. Jude punched up the volume on the flat screen, and they both sat up straight on the sofa, dinner plates forgotten on the coffee table as they both eagerly waited to hear what the leader of the free world had to say. The country was ready for a change at the end of the other President's term. Both political parties, including the lefts and the rights, had become disillusioned over the lack of leadership and the weakened military condition which had basically rendered America vulnerable. No matter which side of the fence they were on, any party, things changed when it was their own cities being attacked; their families being blown apart.

All of a sudden, big military and big guns were a "good thing." At first, President Harrison was a welcome change. He was of mega-military mentality, heavy on artillery, light on tolerance. But it didn't take long for all the criticisms to start up. Since his inauguration, he had been too bogged down in the White House with the nuclear threats and trying to build the military force to address the nation, except to take office. (It didn't sit too well with the Mitlows, either, that he hadn't even bothered to place his hand on the Bible when he was sworn in.) It had only been a couple of other times when the temporary martial law was invoked that he had made a public appearance.

This was like no other time in history. America was under siege! They could hear and feel the battle cry in every land. Some nations were struggling, some rising to power. America was somewhere in between.

"We the people," he quoted in a loud voice, directly from the Constitution in dignitary fashion, pausing at the appropriate time for applause. He continued on to reassure the nation that as the war continued raging, we would defend our country at all costs. He assured the American people that every attack had been met with great resistance and the country was in no way ready to flounder.

Everybody knew that was a load. It felt more like the Titanic after it split in half, but before it sank, bobbing in the dark, murky waters with no place to go but down.

Criticisms were coming in from every direction. With so many troops deployed overseas, people felt vulnerable. Public polls complained there wasn't enough fortitude on American shores. The proof? Terrorist attacks were continuing, and they were as life-altering, if not quadrupled, as they were on 9/11. Only now, not just in New York City and at the Pentagon; it was nationwide. In addition to foreign attacks, there was the definite smell of civil uprising in the air. Americans were great at attacking each other, too, when things got bad. They would get up on their soapboxes and cry for peace, when in reality, they were the ones stirring the proverbial pot. Every state, from Texas to North Dakota, as well as California, was all being affected by the bombings and the infiltration of terrorist cell pods. It was beginning to feel like Jude and her family, as well as the rest of the nation, were all living in another country. With the temporary martial law enforcement, it felt something akin to Communistic rule. There had never been more chaos. It was hard to wrap their minds around it all. Old Beautiful was suffering like never before.

Jackson and Jude listened as the President spoke of law and order, and both perked up when he addressed the sudden presence of all the men in Black Suits. They had been sent to every city, he said, to follow up on the census. Citizens were instructed to comply with them as they were acting on the direct order of the Secret Service. "What do you think, son? Is it about to come apart? You're being awfully quiet." She muted the television after she had determined that anything of great importance had already been said.

Jackson leaned forward with both forearms on his knees and looked down, picking a torn cuticle from his thumb. "I think that something catastrophic is about to happen, Mother," he said. "I heard today through my own sources that China is about to call all of our notes due after they demand that the world oil market dollar is no longer to be held in American currency. If they do this; if they all agree; it'll start a worldwide panic. Then everybody else will call them in too, and that will virtually render all of our money instantly worthless. An economic collapse of such magnitude ...." He paused and looked up at her. "We'd never recover as a nation. We'd never recover. It'd just be ... done," he said, throwing both hands up.

Jude shrank back in disbelief as a shiver ran down her spine. "Oh, my Father God, send Your Son to come get us!" she blurted out. "It feels like the rise of the Antichrist."

Jackson remained as calm as he could, but he was as wound up as she was. He reached over and grabbed her hand and gave it a squeeze. "Mother, you know the Antichrist won't rise to power until we have been raptured out. We won't have to go through that. I can't even imagine how bad all of THIS is even going to get. But I think he is groomed and ready to go. It's starting to feel like we're living in a movie."

He stopped and shook his head as he thought of something else. "It blows my mind to think about the remote cities that haven't been bombed or attacked yet. They're just going about their normal life, going to work, eating dinner, tossing a ball around in the yard like the whole world isn't about to blow up. It's like a frog being boiled in a pot of water. It doesn't realize the temperature's rising until it's too late. But back to the Antichrist. I definitely think he is alive and waiting to make his debut."

"I'm inclined to agree with you. People need to wake up," she said. "It feels like we're on the cusp of something we can't even imagine."

"Agreed," he replied. "I really think we're close."

Jude just nodded sadly as she looked intently at her son. "I know we both know the Scriptures, but let's look at them again, together— like right now." Jackson got up immediately and took the Bible off of the coffee table. They had Bibles in every room. This was the big 40-pound "living room" family Bible. They chose to read out of it on serious occasions. Grayson and Jude had raised their children in the Word. Each one of them had their own relationship with Christ.

"Let's go to the kitchen, Mom. Grab a pen. Nevermind, here, use this one," he said, handing her a black ballpoint pen he produced out of nowhere. "And where is Jessica?" he asked, concerned, as he sat down and grabbed a crisp, green apple from the crystal fruit bowl. Jude put her reading glasses on.

"She's on her way," she assured him, as she got a paring knife out of the silverware drawer and grabbed the shaker of salt. "She called earlier and said a lot had happened today—bad things, but she'll be here."

She scooted her barstool next to his and cored and sliced the apple while discussing what they were reading. They continued through the Bible verses together and regained their footing. "I want to be able to share this with my friends and people at the funeral home," Jude said, as she got up to discard the apple core and a few stray seeds. "How long do you think we will continue to have a normal life? Like, go to work and to the market with all of this going on around us?"

"I don't know," said Jackson, shaking his head. "I have no earthly idea. I get it that you want to share information with your friends, but be careful, Mom. How well do you really know those people down there at the funeral home? Even the owner; we don't really know anything about him, that Daniel 'what's his name.' *("Well,"* thought Jude, *"that might be changing. But for now, I'll keep that to myself.")* Seriously, you could be arrested if the wrong person hears you talk about any of this." He looked at her in her reading glasses with the concern etched in her face. He hated seeing her like this—rattled. It wasn't like her.

"First, let's look at this all realistically," he said, holding both hands like he was measuring width. "Let's talk about the time sequences. We are definitely living in the last days. Here," he said, flipping the thin pages over to Matthew 24:7. He turned the Bible around so she could read it out loud.

MATTHEW 24:7 (NKJV)
"For nation will rise against nation, and kingdom against kingdom. And there will be famines, pestilences, and earthquakes in various places."

She looked up nodding. "And there you have it," she said.

"Yes, ma'am, and we also have the signs in the skies—the Blood Moons. And remember, Israel became a nation in one day back in 1948. That's prophecy fulfilled right out of the book of Ezekiel," Jackson said, as they flipped the worn pages from verse to verse.

She took her glasses off and lightly laid her hand on his. "Let me ask you this before we continue. What happens if it all breaks loose and we're not together, you and me and Jess? What if the bombs go off here in Colleyville and Bedford? Or worse, what if all the nukes get fired? I know it sounds unrealistic, but it makes me want to stay glued to your side," she said, with her voice sounding a little uneasy.

"You're the toughest woman I know, Mother. You've never backed down from anything. We'll figure it out the best we can. I'll get to you if it is humanly possible. You know I will. We have our safe place if we need that, too. I have another couple of things in mind we'll talk about later." He placed his hands on her shoulders. "Mother," he said firmly, "you're going to be all right, regardless. I know you." He held up three fingers and counted them down as he made each point. "You love the Lord; you trust Him. No matter what happens to any of us, it's all going to work out in the end. And if something does happen to me, you keep it together. Promise me that."

She had let her tough façade down for just a moment, and her eyes sparkled with tears. "I love you, sweetheart—you and your sister. I just don't want anything to happen to either of you," she whispered, clasping both hands over her heart as she looked up at him. "I just don't think I could survive it. I wouldn't want to." Neither one of them could say anything. They both choked up with emotion as the unknown lay before them. He hugged her as she struggled to gather her composure. And she did. Jude was a strong woman. She could do this. She had no other choice.

Chapter 11

An Explosion

Jessica came barreling in during their heartfelt moment. Jude quickly brushed the tears from her cheek putting on a brave face. Jessica had quite the story! The Black Suits swarmed the courthouse earlier that morning after a nearby explosion. They had forcefully blocked her in the hall to search the cardboard box full of files she was carrying. They unceremoniously had dumped and pilfered through its contents. Then they just left everything scattered on the floor. "If it hadn't been for this 40-pound watermelon I've got strapped on," she said, motioning to her belly, flailing her arms around practically with made-up gang signs as she bobbed her head from side to side, "I would have given them 'what for!'"

Jackson and Jude listened on while the rest of the story unfolded. She was furious! She had decided it was over. It was no longer safe to be in downtown Dallas. The streets were overrun with cops and soldiers trying to keep a handle on the city. A homemade scud had found its way into the wrong hands, and it had deployed itself in a hotel garage, blowing up half of South Lamar for blocks! The DPS had sectioned off a mile or so to make way for the fire trucks and ambulances as they removed bodies and transported the injured to the county hospital with sirens blaring all over the city. This, combined with the masses moving deeper downtown now, homeless and fleeing from the threat of another explosion, left Jessica to arrive at only one conclusion. She had packed up her office and fled the courthouse. That's when the Suits had stopped her. Her pregnant belly didn't elicit any kind of compassion from them; they could have cared less.

"I looked them right in the eyes," exclaimed Jessica. "My stranger danger went bonkers! Their eyes seemed vacant, like they had no soul!"

They both got stirred up just listening to her tell it. It had taken her two and a half hours just to get on Hwy 183. The traffic was jammed up for miles. Jackson was pacing by this point, worried for his sister, knowing he was powerless to go back and do anything about it.

While Jessica finished telling them of the harrowing events, Jude made her an egg white scramble and peach smoothie. Jude was so thankful she had made it home safely. She didn't say it aloud, but as she looked at both her children while they discussed the explosion, the Black Suits and the Presidential speech, she wondered if they would all make it through this alive. She kept these things to herself as she headed up the stairs to get a bath. She pinned her hair up in a big silver clip and poured lavender bath salts in the running water. She filled it to the rim and sank deep into the warm, comforting water and wondered what would become of her beloved family.

Chapter 12

You've Got Mail

The days had grown warmer, and the yard was now showing bold displays of early summer colors. Bright red geraniums lined the walkway along with yellow cannas and stalks of purple lavender. Spring had come and gone already by early May. The grass was a beautiful, dark green. Irises and daffodils had come briefly, showing off their glorious colors of blues and yellows, and then once again retreated to the rich, dark earth from which they came. They were replaced by cheery patches of white periwinkles with pink eyes and winding vines of blue morning glories and late evening moon flowers with their showy white blooms. The lofty branches of the trees had waved and swayed in the gentle morning breezes, totally unaware of the world around them.

The earth and all nature had no idea of the ugliness surrounding it. The riots had left once pretty courtyards in the city littered with debris. The looting and fires had done their damage as well. In addition to the obvious, the military marching through the soot that the helicopters rained down every evening had left the streets and sidewalks filthy. But here at Jude's home, she continued to water and prune and make it as pretty as possible.

Several weeks had passed since the Presidential speech and the incident at the courthouse. Jessica was still tying up a few loose ends from her practice using a courier service. She never went back to Dallas again. Jackson had been in and out of the gym, but still successfully dodged the census.

Jude had carved out a little fledgling relationship with Daniel at the funeral home and become easily acquainted with Spencer as well. The world was still topsy-turvy, straining under the heavy arm of the government. They were pressing in hard with more rules and regulations (mainly no public demonstrations or proclaiming Christianity). Why they were blaming the Christians, nobody knew. They claimed it was temporary. They said Christianity instigated cultural unrest. That was the best they could come up with.

Jude and her family stuck close to the house these days. Jessica was draggy with her "40-pound kid" strapped to her waist as she called it. Jude and Jackson went to work and then straight home.

When Jude came in the door one evening, she noticed Jessica was on the sofa with her feet propped up. "Jessica? You okay?" she asked.

"My back's killing me. It's been hurting off and on all day," she said, sounding irritated.

Jude jumped to attention. "Do we need to go to the hospital?"

"No, Mom, it's not like that. I'm just uncomfortable. It aches if I sit up too long."

Jude leaned over and placed her hand on Jessica's brow.

"Mom, I don't have a fever. I'm pregnant."

"I know. I was just making sure you weren't coming down with the flu or anything." Jessica reached up and placed her hand over her mother's hand. It did feel oddly soothing to her. *"Mother's soft, cool hand on my forehead, like when I was a kid,"* she thought.

"Well, you got some mail," said Jude, as she handed an official-looking letter addressed to Jessica from CAFA. (She had wanted to rip it open in the driveway and read it herself, but that being a felony and all, she didn't want those nosy neighbors reporting it.) Jessica said the Suits still came regularly, but nothing new. No more flashes of lights from the windows were seen either.

Jessica took the letter and ran her finger under the seal and tossed the empty envelope on the coffee table. She snapped the fold out of the letter with a flick of her wrist and struggled to sit up as she continued reading in a half mumble and then just let the letter hang in her hand. "No surprise here," she said, as she waved it. "They discovered Tony's Special Ops rendezvous location, and they have informed him of the baby. That was it. That was the entire letter. As usual, not a peep out of him; not even about his child."

Jessica, feeling a little irritated, pitched the letter over with the envelope. Her feelings for him had begun to change over the last seven months. She had totally lost any respect for him. Would she want a father for her son who ran when things got difficult? A father who left the country just because he decided he didn't want to live in America anymore? His being gone might be the best, at least for now, but he had the right to know about the kid, and she had done her part.

"Well, at least you told him," said Jude, sympathetically. "He's had time to digest it. I wouldn't worry about it for now. We have more important things to consider, like keeping you healthy."

Jude checked the crockpot she had left that morning, and the roast was tender and the smell was intoxicating. She set the table, then went upstairs to grab a quick rinse and change out of her funeral suit. Jackson came in and chunked his keys on the bar and flopped down in the living room with Jessica.

"Where's Mom?" he asked, looking around. "She made it home yet?"

"Yeah," she replied, "she's upstairs changing for dinner."

"Man, I could smell that roast from the driveway," Jackson said, rubbing his stomach in anticipation. They both loved her cooking, but Jessica crinkled up her nose.

"Yeah, I've smelled it all day long, to the point of nausea. Don't tell Mom. I think she made it for me."

"Yeah, don't mess with her cooking," he said, "she'll skin you alive." They both chuckled lightheartedly and got up when they heard her coming down the stairs.

Jackson held out his hand to his sister and pulled her up, moaning and groaning like he was moving a couch. "Thanks," she said, in a flat tone. He just smirked as they both pitched in with tea and butter for the rolls and headed into the dining room.

They shared light conversation, enjoying the food she had prepared—all of their normal Sunday fare, but they were having this on Thursday. Pot roast, potatoes and carrots, sautéed green beans, buttered corn and hot rolls (Jessica's favorites).

Jessica had managed to choke down a potato and a roll. She wasn't very hungry tonight. She left the table to go back to the couch before they finished. She felt miserable.

"You want a scoop of ice cream, Jessica?" Jude asked, following her to make sure she was okay. "That's all I have for dessert tonight."

"That's fine, Mom, but I think I'll pass. I'm just not feeling it today."

"Jessica, would you know if you needed to go to the hospital?" she asked again. "Do you think it's back labor?"

"Mom, come on. I promise it's not labor. It just feels like I lifted something too heavy. Trust me, if I thought this kid was trying to come out, I'd be driving myself to the hospital, administering my own drugs. I'm not the 'all natural' type. I hate pain."

"Okay, I'll quit bugging you," Jude said, with her hand on her hip. "I'm just worried, that's all." Jude headed back into the dining room where Jackson was still eating.

"I had to go through two stop checks on the way home this evening," she told him, as she scooped frozen ice cream into two dessert dishes.

"What are they checking for? You mean the Police? My buddy said they are comparing driver's licenses to census reporting for accuracy. At least, that's what the word on the street is," he said, taking the scooper from her to add more to his dish.

"Oh, my. I hope you don't get pulled over," Jude said, looking worried.

"Don't worry, Mom. I've been very, very careful. If they catch me, they catch me. But for now, I think I've been able to avoid them pretty well."

"It's the first time it's happened to me," said Jude, as she took a small bite of her ice cream. "And then twice in one day! It shook me up. I thought my Bible was on the back seat."

Jackson looked up from his bowl. "Well, it's not against the new regulation to have a Bible."

"But wait," she said, "they did say in the letter you could have no public conversations about it. So I just wasn't sure if the actual Bible was okay."

"It's so ridiculous," he said, starting to get irritated, "but I know what you mean. No sense in deliberately pushing the envelope."

"Speaking of envelopes, did Jessica tell you about the letter she got about Tony?"

"No, she didn't say anything, but you know what? I could have sworn I saw him today—just for a second. I did a double take on a guy who looked like him talking to one of the Black Suit guys in the coffee shop by my gym. He disappeared, so I couldn't get a good look at him. But I swear it looked just like him."

"That's odd," said Jude. "Why would he be here and not immediately find Jessica? The letter said he had been informed about the baby."

"I don't know," he said, shaking his head, "but I'd like the chance to relieve him of some of his teeth."

"Well, don't say that in front of her tonight. She feels bad enough."

"I won't, Mom," he assured her. "I'm just stomping and snorting around about it. After everything he's put her through and now this."

"I know, son. I feel the same, but for tonight, let's just catch the news and get a good night's rest."

Chapter 13

And the Earth Quaked

The sound was deafening. Like a roaring freight train crashing through the bricks! It cracked and groaned and screeched as if the house was being torn asunder! The walls were quaking, and pictures were shaken from the hooks that had held them for years. Glasses and cups came crashing out of the cabinets while pots and pans rattled and swung from their pot hangers as the house shook unrelentingly! Jude was trying to clamor her way out of a deep sleep, clawing at the darkness behind her eyelids. As she was trying to wake up, instinct told her to take cover! She was jolted awake as the huge painting of magnolias above her bed came crashing down over her! Her brain kept trying to process! The power of whatever was happening held her down on the bed as it moved and shook violently like a scene out of *The Exorcist! Are we being bombed?*

"Oh, dear God, help us!" Jude screamed, but nothing could be heard over the sound of the roar! Her nightstand toppled over, glass shattering into a thousand pieces! The TV swung and bobbed on its wall mount as the bowels of the earth shifted its plates. It creaked and moaned like something ancient rising from the depths of the ocean. Then it stopped … nothing … dead in its tracks. She was frozen under the painting. The only sound was the creaking of the TV mount in its final swing.

She trembled as she tried to gather her bearings, struggling to move the 60-pound framed painting. *"Oh, no! The kids,"* she thought. She shouted Jessica's name and stepped out of her bed. Immediately, she felt something sharp pierce her foot. "Jackson!" she screamed, as she fell back on her bed! "Jessica!" She had to get to the hall. "Please, somebody!" she cried, "can you hear me?"

Her eyes adjusted in the twilight and she could make out her slippers still lying close to the bed like a divine appointment next to the tall, cut glass reading lamp that had broken in half and crashed into the end table. She stretched one of her legs out and picked up the blue slipper with her toes and brought it up to her hand. She felt it for shards of glass and then slipped it on along with the other one, blood oozing out of the shoe and on to the white carpet. She didn't care! She wanted to get to her children. First, she heard Jessica. Faint, muffled. But it was her.

"Mother! Are you okay?"

"Mom! Can you hear us?" shouted Jackson.

Jessica asked him, "Hey, are *you* okay?" Jude could hear them both talking now.

"I'm okay—I think," Jackson said, as he started feeling the blood trickle down his cheek!

"Is everyone all right? Is anybody hurt?" Jude shouted, making her way to the bedroom door. Her room was turned completely upside down. Two heavy overstuffed chairs had slid across the floor and were stacked, blocking the bedroom doors. The huge flower arrangement of blue hydrangeas had skated off the heavy antique dresser and laid scattered everywhere. "Do the lights still work?" she asked loudly through the doors.

"Yes!" they both answered at once as she heaved and struggled with the chairs holding her prisoner.

"I can't get out," she said, in a brief moment of pending hysteria, yanking and pushing on the chairs. Jackson had gotten to the hall and was bleeding from both knees.

Jessica stared wide-eyed, still freaked out.

"Oh, my gosh, Jackson! You're bleeding!"

He glanced down at his knees, both dripping blood. "I was battling against the quaking to get to you guys. The force just kept slamming me to my knees! I've never felt so helpless in all my life!" he said, choking on his own emotion, relieved he had made it upstairs.

"What?! Who's bleeding?" Jude shouted, beginning to feel desperate to get out.

"Why isn't Mom coming out of her room?" Jackson asked, afraid for her. "Mother!" he shouted again!

He made his way to her room and could hear her struggling on the other side of the heavy double doors.

"Get away from the doors!" he shouted, running on pure adrenalin.

"Wait!" Jude cried out. "There's two chairs blocking them. Don't hurt your shoulder. Let me try and move one of them."

As she strained against the weight of the chairs, he was pushing and forcing the door open inch by inch until he could see her barely through the four-inch opening he had made. She had blood on her face matting the silver streak on her temple where it was already trying to clot. He went in to overdrive pushing and yelling for all he was worth, and the chairs finally moved. It gave him enough room to reach through and push them the remaining way.

"Mom," he said, with an alarmed look on his face because of all the blood. She had tears coming down her face by now, too, and sheetrock in her hair. She reached out for him and grabbed both of his hands, helping him forward over the rubble. She was so grateful he was able to get the doors open.

"Your knees, Jackson!" she gasped.

"Mom, your face has blood on it. I think it's superficial though."

"Don't worry about me, Jackson, let me see your knees." They were chewed like raw hamburger meat. "How's your sister? Where is she? Is she hurt, too?"

"She looks fine physically. She was out in the hall. I told her not to move. There's broken glass everywhere. She didn't listen to me, of course. She went to her room anyway and has been digging around for her tennis shoes," Jackson said, as he helped his mother to the door so she could see for herself.

Jessica was a sight for sore eyes. Debris in her tousled hair, but no visible blood or injuries. She just stood there in her white yogas and her pink shorty shirt, and yes, she had found her shoes. It looked pitiful with her standing there, a protective hand over her big, ballooned belly.

"Oh, gosh," Jude said in a whisper, as she looked at the size of the swollen abdomen and then at Jackson. "She's really pregnant!"

"Uhhhh, yeah, Mom, she is."

"Are you all right, Jessica?"

"I think I'm fine, Mom, but let's bandage both of you," she said, as she saw the bright red blood staining the carpet.

Jessica found the bandages and alcohol and laid them out.

"It was an earthquake," Jackson told them, helping his mother to the bathroom. "In Colleyville, Texas, no less!"

Jude looked shocked. "I swear, I thought it was a bomb."

"I'll bet it was at least a 4.0," said Jackson. "Once I do what I can here, I'll venture out and see what the rest of the city looks like and check the gym. But first, we need to check your head and foot and my knees."

"Jessica? Are you sure you're okay?"

"Yeah, I'm fine, Mom. I'm just stunned I think."

They cleaned and wrapped their wounds and made their way down the staircase. Some rooms were worse than others. Some looked untouched at all. There were potted plants knocked over, dirt and sheetrock powder everywhere.

"All the walls are still intact, I think," said Jackson. "Just some cracks, and we still have a roof over our heads." They went room to room as they made their way into the kitchen and dining room.

Jessica noted the broken dishes. "Mom, you're going to be upset. Most of Mimi's tea set is out on the floor. There are only about five cups left unbroken at this point." Jude shook her head, put her hand over her mouth and fought back the tears. She was heartbroken over her mother's treasured cups. She squatted down, trying to fit the pieces of china together when the doorbell rang. Jackson made his way into the living room and to the front of the house. It was Daniel.

"Yes?" Jackson said, as he opened the door. Daniel stuck out his hand. "I'm Daniel, from the funeral home. I'm sorry to barge in, but I couldn't stop myself. I had to know if you guys were okay."

"Daniel, the doctor? Funeral home guy?" Jackson asked, confused.

"Yes, well, I'm not actually a doctor. I was an Army medic." He was trying to look past Jackson as he answered, but that was impossible. Jackson was taking up the whole doorframe on purpose. "But I can certainly help you guys, and by the looks of your bandaged knees, I've come just in time." They both looked down at the blood that was oozing out of one of the bandages. "But first, where's Jude?" he asked, trying to be polite but wanting to burst forth going room to room until he found her.

Jackson finally moved and let him in the house, and they made their way through the rubble and found Jude still crouched on the floor over her mother's broken china. She still had the blood matted at her temple, the rest of her dark hair was cascading around her shoulders, and she was still in her night clothes. He noted an obvious foot injury. Her bandage was blood soaked, too.

When she looked up and saw Daniel, she was caught between being surprised and she didn't know what else, but whatever it was, it stole her voice. She couldn't utter a word. She tried to stand but stumbled. Both men reflexed instantly and reached out for her at the same time, but her eyes were on Daniel. He tried to help her to steady herself, but she was having trouble gaining her balance. Daniel just swooped her up like she didn't weigh ten pounds and looked at Jackson standing there with his mouth open in silent protest.

"Where can I take her?" he said, with authority. Jackson, a little shocked at the "Rhett Butler and Scarlett O'Hara" scene guided him to the living room and snatched a throw to lay her on. Even in this mess, he knew his mother wouldn't want to get blood on the sofa. He watched Daniel cautiously as he handled his mother, who seemed to be quite comfortable being carried from room to room, arms draped around this guy's neck. Jessica appeared out of nowhere. Daniel glanced down at the pregnancy. "You okay, sweetie?"

Jessica glanced at Jackson, then at her mother. "I'm fine. Who are you, and what are you doing with my mother?" she said, in a monotone voice.

Jackson stepped in. "This is Daniel from the funeral home," he informed her. "He was a medic."

"I know. The Army doctor," Jessica retorted.

Jude was embarrassed at both of them already knowing that about him—obviously from her revelation.

"Yes, that's me," he said, not even glancing at Jude. (He was happy to know at least she had talked about him.) "Now, let's get you guys checked out." He turned to Jessica. "First, are you sure you're fine? The baby good? Any bleeding? Any cramps?" he asked Jessica.

Jessica pulled her head back a little at the personal questions, but then shrugged her shoulders and answered him. "I'm not hurt anywhere, and from the kicking, he's doing fine, too," she said, rubbing her belly.

"Then my son, Spencer, is in the car. Will you go get him and tell him to bring my medical bag please? I brought it just in case. I didn't know what to expect when I got here."

"Sure," said Jessica, as she headed toward the front door.

Daniel's military background was playing out right there in their living room, barking orders and sending people on errands. He was "on the job" and somehow it was okay. They just did what he asked. If their mom felt comfortable, they'd go along.

Jessica made her way out to the front just as Spencer was getting out of the car, already wondering what was taking his dad so long.

"Are you Spencer?" she asked, shielding her eyes with her hand from the sun that had just come up fully.

"That would be me," he said, noticing her abdomen in full view and smudged as she was still in her short shirt (now filthy from the rubble dust indoors).

"Your dad said he wants you to grab his bag thingy. My mom's hurt and so is my brother."

Spencer immediately grabbed the bag and hurried behind her dirty yoga pants to check on Jude. He hadn't known Jude too long, but long enough for him to care about her and be concerned that she was hurt.

He followed Jessica in. She turned slightly and said, "By the way, I'm Jessica."

"I figured as much," he answered. "Your mom talks about y'all a lot at work, although she didn't mention a baby." Jessica just looked up at him. About that time, Jackson filled the entrance of the living room, arms akimbo. Spencer grinned, one eyebrow up. "Seriously?" he said, at Jackson's size.

"I get that a lot," said Jackson, already knowing the meaning of the comment. "Jackson," he introduced himself to Spencer, sticking out his hand.

"Spencer," Spencer replied, jamming his own hand out. Spencer was tall, too, and they looked eye to eye as they sized each other up for a brief moment, both gripping the handshake (not enough to crush the other's hand, but tight enough). Jackson stepped aside and both went to the sofa where Jude and Daniel were.

"Spencer," Jude said from the couch. "You met my family?"

"I did. What did you do in here? Lose your temper?" he joked, looking around at the disaster. They all chuckled. "It's all fun and games until somebody loses a house." Jackson liked him right away. Dry humor, quick-witted, just like him and Jessica.

"Oh, sorry, we didn't bother to even ask you guys," said Jackson, looking back and forth from Daniel to Spencer. "Did y'all get any damage? How's the funeral home?"

Daniel was quick to answer as he finished cleaning the small cut on Jude's temple. "In Aurora—that's where we live—we didn't get any damage. We just felt slight rumblings. The funeral home, however, suffered some broken glass and some displaced caskets in the selection room, but thankfully, everything stayed underground in the cemetery, if you know what I mean."

Jude, for one, was horrified at the alternative to that last statement! "I'm so happy everything is still, 'Operational'," she replied. "Glad it wasn't worse. I thought for sure we had been bombed."

"So did we," said Daniel. "That could actually be next. Let's just thank God it wasn't."

Daniel lifted her foot. She was embarrassed as he gently unwrapped it with Jackson, Spencer and Jessica staring. Her foot was dirty by now. Thank goodness she had her toenails done recently. She didn't want to suffer any further embarrassment with such an intimate encounter with her foot.

"Jackson," she said, "why don't you and Spencer go check the patio while we get this foot tended to." Jude glanced down to see if any of her toenails had been torn or snagged. "Then I want Daniel to check your knees."

"My knees are fine, Mom. Do you want me to find your robe?" he asked her, noticing she was still in her pale blue nightshirt.

"I'm just fine," Jude said, raising an eyebrow at him—her signal for "shut it."

"Okay. I'll check the patio. Then I'm going to try to get to the gym and see what the rest of the streets look like. Wanna ride?" Jackson asked, looking at Spencer.

"Sure," he answered, then unconsciously glanced over at Jessica. "Just drop me off at the funeral home after."

"Okay," said Jackson, and they took off. Moments later, they started texting photos. It was a mess everywhere. The nosy neighbor's house was visibly damaged; the residential streets, some broken open; Hwy 26 was split for a good city block; water hydrants shooting water 30 feet high. There were buildings sagging, sirens blaring everywhere. But the gym, like a miracle, was untouched. Nothing. Not even a shattered window pane. The Black Suits were out in full force. The military was pitching in with local police trying to contain the disaster. Colleyville would never be the same.

Chapter 14

The Cleanup and a Spy

It took weeks to clean and repair the house from the aftermath of the earthquake. The house and yard were a conglomeration of sawhorses, hammers and electric saws, accompanied by bright orange extension cords snaking a path out of the opened garage.

The inside, much to Jude's chagrin, likewise hosted several buckets filled with beige and pale blue paints, drop cloths, brushes, rollers and blanket-covered pictures stacked in various locations. The china cups that had survived were hung back on their hooks. The rest of the broken pieces were saved in a small box to be later used in a mosaic table. *"That will probably never even be started,"* she thought.

Jude, standing in her bedroom in a pair of white capris and a blue and white stripe tank top, was holding a drippy roller extension. She looked around, satisfied. The second coat was applied evenly. Jessica brought in a glass of iced tea and giggled at the sight of her mom performing manual labor, not to mention her hair being twisted into some kind of a lumpy knot and in biblical proportion due to the humidity and sweat.

Jude had hired out most of the construction of the repairs to a couple of handymen she had used for years. The rest, her and Jackson had done with the much appreciated help of Daniel and Spencer. They had swept, cleaned carpets and filled black trash bags full of debris. After the last load was hauled off, they celebrated with steaks on the grill that had survived the deep freezer being temporarily on the blink. Then they divvied up projects that had to be completed. Daniel and Jude had tried to do all of their projects together. He had come in his jeans and painter's shirt under the pretense of "checking up" on her and Jackson's wounds but had immediately pitched in and helped. He had taped everything off for them and had put all of the drop cloths out.

He came as often as he could, bearing gifts of sugary donuts and paper cups filled with designer coffees. He still had a business to run and much to his disappointment, he couldn't stay all day. Neither could Spencer with the government requiring body removals from all of the jails. He stayed more than Daniel though. He, too, had enjoyed working side by side with them and getting to know them all better.

Jessica was the appointed tea and beverage waitress and all things lunch. The guys did all of the heavy lifting, such as cans of soda and slices of ice-cold watermelon. They mainly gave instructions to the handymen and tried to reserve the fun stuff for themselves like all things related to power tools and demolition, while sporting motorcycle club "do-rags," jeans and no shirts. Jessica had made many, many trips to where they were working. She might be pregnant, but she wasn't blind. Spencer—well, she liked the way his pockets looked on his jeans. She acted like she could care less about him with his constant teasing and pet names he randomly chose for her, such as "pregs," "straps" or "nurse." She hated them all—or at least pretended to.

Chapter 15

The Eyes Upon Us

Colleyville was a huge mess. It was hard to maneuver around all of the orange cones and sinkholes. The patrons of the gym were scattered, almost down to nothing. More than once, Jackson had contemplated permanently locking the doors. He was having more and more difficulty dodging the authorities. He mainly slipped off early in the mornings on his bike before they got started on the house projects, checked everything out and tried for new sightings of Tony. He had left his SUV at the funeral home while he and Spencer had gone scouting around and never returned to get it. They both had fast bikes and wore dark glasses and helmets, and so far, Jackson had managed to stay under the radar. If they were ever riding together and saw any official vehicles, Jackson pulled his bike away from Spencer's like they weren't together. So far, it had worked.

Jessica had survived her backaches and was getting closer to her final month. The guys teased her about her growing waistline after she polished off an entire ribeye and baked sweet potato. She instantly grabbed a dinner roll and shoved the whole thing in her mouth to make a point. She'd eat everything that wasn't nailed down if she felt like it.

She blamed it on the "40 lb. strap-on kid;" however, it looked to them like the kid was innocent. Jessica could put away more food these days than either one of them they had teased. She only weighed 126 lbs. before the pregnancy and was now only topping the scales around 140, even at nearing full-term, but she was all baby. It really did look like a 40 lb. watermelon.

Even with all of the home repairs, they were always in earshot of the news and their surroundings. They never escaped from what was going on around them, like a top spinning that could go off the table at any moment. The government's control and the new laws were always their main topics of conversation. Things were getting more and more tense everywhere. Even though they hated the intrusion of the government personally, they all agreed it kept the voice of the public down to a soft roar. They weren't faced with the daily rioting and confusion that the bigger cities were dealing with, but it was getting closer; they could just feel it. Nobody in their actual subdivision or any of their friends had been arrested for a crime or breaking the speech laws, just a client at Jackson's gym and a new guy at the funeral home. It was always a friend of a friend, friend's second cousin, someone they had barely heard of. Little did they know this was all about to change.

Tony, Jessica's estranged husband, wearing a ball cap and dark glasses, crouched around the side of the nosy neighbor's house, spying on the Mitlows. He was watching through a pair of binoculars. He could see almost everything from his hiding spot. He shifted the crotch of his jeans and squatted down. He watched in disgust as Jessica presented a glass of iced tea on a serving tray to a strange, shirtless guy in her mom's front yard. He glanced down at the stack of census reports he was holding as he wiped beads of sweat from his upper lip, wondering who he was. He wondered why Jackson's name wasn't on one either. He knew he was bound to be here. He was a "momma's boy" from what he remembered. He never could stand Jackson. He'd find him. He had seen him hanging around the gym a couple of times since he'd gotten back into town on assignment. He didn't know why he hadn't reported him yet, but he would—all in due time.

"They never liked me," he thought to himself. *"None of them! Thought I wasn't good enough for Jessica—and maybe I wasn't, but who do they think they are? I'm glad Grayson is dead—arrogant so and so! He tried to turn Jessica against me from the beginning."* "Good riddance old man!" he said out loud with pure hatred in his voice. "And I hope Jude is devastated.

What a prude she is." He changed the position of his squat. His stupid leg was starting to cramp.

He didn't know who the shirtless stranger was and really didn't care, but he could see her bulging belly. *"Is it even mine?"* he wondered. He was gone for months. They had sent him to Iran on a special mission months ago. He knew he had made a mistake seeing her after her dad died—a moment of weakness. Now he really regretted it. He wasn't interested in starting a family—ever! She dang well knew it, too! He had trained for months on end, and he wasn't about to let her change that. *Why did she even keep the kid in the first place? She said she didn't want babies either. Careless idiot! I should have stuck something in my wallet!*

He was sent back here after training to head up one of the units that identified Christian families who were not obeying the new speech laws—but from a distance until they had enough evidence to accuse them of something. It was his job to round them up, bring them in, make them give up the names of others they knew who couldn't keep their mouths shut about a book full of lies they had built their whole lives around. What a bunch of morons. He even did some of the interrogations—which he truly enjoyed. He loved to see people sweat, squirm, scream as he used any means necessary to get the information he needed. He'd love to get Jude in there. By the time he was finished with her, she'd tell him where Jackson was and anything else he wanted to know. Smug witch.

He got off thinking about it. He loved this new life of his. He didn't need a smart-mouthed woman and snot-nosed, squalling brat clinging to him, holding him back. He was loyal to no one. He had plans to go up. All the way up! To the very top of CAFA. Nobody was going to stop him! Nobody was going to trap him! The only one who was going to be setting any traps was him. He'd trap them all. Add a few stars to his uniform. And he couldn't wait to haul Jackson in and listen to him screaming for his momma. That would be a glorious day, he fantasized, and smiled. He was afraid he'd laugh right out loud and give away his hiding place. Just the thought of hauling them all in really turned him on. They were so prim and proper. Ha! He stood up and nursed his cramping calf, then he slipped back out of view and headed back to his car that was hidden around the corner. He got back to headquarters and made his plans. He had talked secretly to his Aunt Lucy at the funeral home several times about keeping tabs on Jude for months now. Next time, he'd ask her about the shirtless wonder. All in good time. He'd take his good sweet time about it. Fools. He'd put them in their self-righteous places once and for all, and enjoy doing it!

Chapter 16

Rules

The helicopters swarmed overhead, going back and forth from the Lake Worth base to the base over by Camp Carter. The executive order limiting expressed speech and political views other than those of the White House were now being enforced nationwide. Zero tolerance. The Camps were becoming more noticeable now as they had put them in every city after the jails were filled to capacity. At first, the activists got on their soap boxes and passionately shouted equality for the violated Constitution—but to no avail. They no longer marched with their proverbial flags. They had all been arrested—or worse. The answer to the brave outbursts? Raids. Plenty of whistleblowers. Bad was now good; good was now bad.

The same time every evening, the city sirens went off, 15 minutes prior to curfew call. Then they sounded sharply at 10:00 p.m. Everybody off the streets.

The war raged on. The cities hit the hardest were the bigger ones: Chicago, New York, Los Angeles, Austin and many, many others. The fighting was constant on every part of the map. There was one country, however, giving the appearance of being silent—Germany. History had proven time and again, silent they may be, but they were definitely a super power. America watched, and the media speculated, but nobody knew for sure what they were up to.

The terrorist attacks had not reached Colleyville—close, but not yet. Earthquakes had hit the Mid-cities area and created some aftershocks, but Jude's house didn't receive any more damage. The rumble of the actual war was always there in the background. China hadn't voted on recalling the notes yet, nor had the market money changed from U.S. dollars to the yuan (CNY) or any other suggested foreign currency. The powers that be were still deliberating on establishing a one-world currency, but not yet. The nations still feared the nukes would be deployed at any moment, but they hadn't, not yet. ISIS was still marching, continuing to enlarge in numbers. Things were still escalating around the world. Many nations, cities and providences were burning American flags and chanting obscenities about the country. Murdering and imprisoning American citizens and Christians alike were at a worldwide high. The hatred had worked itself up into a frenzy. They were all coming together like a living organism in a petri dish—growing in number and power.

"Destroy Jerusalem, Jews and Christians!" the world chanted. The camera crews panned the masses showing close-ups of their distorted faces. Every nation! Every tribe! Every language shouted in unison, "Death to the Christians! Death to the Jews! Death to the Americans!" The common hatred of Israel and America was unilateral. Some had blamed the old Presidential regime (to their everlasting shame) for the way the country was now looked upon—weakened, not the super power they once were. The new President was trying his best to turn that around as quickly as possible.

The talk of Armageddon, last days and such broadcasts had all been banned as it caused more dissension. Even the mention of other gods in other religions and their holy books were forbidden. The Bible, the Torah, books of Hindu and Jehovah's Witness—all silenced. The Black Suits were making sure of that. They monitored everything. Cable channels being watched were monitored through surveillance vans in every neighborhood, public phones were tapped, any public speaking monitored. It was hard to tell the good guys from the bad guys in just a matter of a few months.

Most churches had completely disbanded after their ministers had been dragged out from behind their pulpits during their messages on End Times. When they said, "No talk about Christ," they meant it, and they enforced it. They had taken some of the guns and ammunition during the home invasions. The White House was in the process of creating a new gun control law, under the pretense of not hurting each other, but really as a matter of control over the citizens. Render them defenseless—not against the terrorists, against their own government! The media mainly focused on trying to control the public opinions which only seemed to instill more unrest. The jails had filled up so fast and had created such severe overcrowding, the only viable alternative was to enforce eminent domain and begin to use vacant grocery stores and buildings as temporary holding places or "C-Camps," the slang word for Christian Camps. Unless the funeral home came to take away your body, you were never heard from again.

Chapter 17

The Camp

Spencer was the only one certified to go into the Camps to make removals. The Suits had come to the funeral home and laid out regulations for retrieving deceased bodies from the Camps, and it had to be followed to the letter. They had elected Spencer Wayne as the point of contact. He had been sworn to discretion and forbidden to discuss, even with the funeral home, the conditions and what he witnessed in the Camps. Daniel and Jude could see as plain as day that all the women and men alike had their heads shaved when they came in and sores in some cases from lice and unattended wounds. They appeared to be relatively nourished, but some had shown the markings of straps or cuffs on the ankles and hands. Some had unidentified markings as well.

The protocol was always the same. They would call for his services. He would immediately get into the big, black, box van and go. The room where the bodies were held for pickup was right next to the bunkers of the prisoners. He could see them milling around. Their looks— desperate, stripped of dignity. The smell of the close quarters in the hot Texas afternoons was unbearable. A shoddy ventilation system blew the stench of stagnant, overrun restroom filth and human sweat. It was a stench you didn't soon forget.

While still in the Camp, he would have about 10 minutes alone to wrap the body, place it in the removal casket and then signal for a couple of the guards to help get it to the van. He was allowed to bring one person to help load once they got to the van, but that individual couldn't step outside of the van. He would be shot on sight. It was a horrible job for Spencer, but it gave him something, some power, to figure out a way to help. That's why he made nice with the guards. He had even choked on cigarette smoke and pretended to swig some whiskey to stay on their good side. He wanted them to trust him completely. He and his dad were working on a plan. There had to be a way to help these people—to figure out a way to rescue at least some of them. He tried to make a mental layout of the facility and copy down what he saw as soon as he would get down the road while it was still fresh in his mind. Their hollow faces haunted him day and night. He and Daniel thought they had come up with a fairly clever plan; only time would tell. It was risky. It could mean their own deaths, but they had to do something.

Chapter 18

There Goes the Neighborhood

Jude came down the stairs hurriedly in her funeral clothes—black slacks, white silk blouse with lots of silver bracelets. She had chosen practical black pumps for comfort today. The extra hours were starting to take a toll on her feet and apparently her ability to hear the alarm clock.

Still rubbing almond and cherry lotion into her hands, she darted into the laundry room where the deep freezer sat across from the stainless steel washer and dryer. She held it open for a minute while the cold, frosty air escaped. She pulled out a package of pork chops to thaw for dinner, along with a small plastic sandwich bag full of hand-picked berries from last year's bounty. They had a small blackberry bush in the backyard that had been there since they bought the house. Every year, it yielded about 20 bags of berries which they enjoyed with sprinkles of raw sugar or as a topping for homemade ice cream. *"Seems like another lifetime ago,"* she thought, as she glanced at the unused packages. She went back into the kitchen and laid them both on the counter on a platter. "Keep an eye on those today," she said to Jackson, "and stick them in the fridge once they thaw, if you don't mind."

Jackson was sitting at the bar on his first cup of coffee looking at his hand-held mini device.

"Anything happen last night?" she asked him.

"Yeah, there was a raid at the Yoga center over by your funeral home late last night. Said they were having secret meetings there. Something having to do with pamphlets they were trying to get out."

Jude crinkled her nose. "What kind of pamphlets?"

"It doesn't really say. They just said pamphlets," he answered, shaking his head.

She looked over his shoulder. "Wow, that's getting close."

"Yep, it's starting to not look like the Metroplex around here anymore. It's got that feel like you see in the movies of the beginning stages of Nazi, Germany," he said, as he scrolled further down the page and continued reading to himself.

Jude went back to the counter, watching the coffee maker as it began filling her cup. "I was thinking the same thing last night when I went to bed," she said, as she opened a copper canister labeled Sugar. "I always feel like we're being watched—or recorded. I don't know if it's paranoia or it's really happening." She cracked an egg in the nonstick skillet and neither one of them said anything else.

Jude pulled out of the garage as the sun had just begun to peek over the rooftops, blinking in and out through the gray, cloudy sky. *"Looks like rain today,"* she thought, as she saw a flash of lightning in the distance, followed by far-away thunder. It was still cool and quiet in the neighborhood. It was going to be a busy day. Her coffee was in a cheerful, pink polka dot travel mug, and she was holding a fried egg sandwich wrapped in a paper napkin. She hadn't fed the birds this morning. Everything had changed environmentally. She didn't know if it was the thick fog that always hung overhead now, or the birds knew something they didn't. They were scarce, nearly all gone.

The residential streets had all been repaired since the quake. Now they were dotted with surveillance vans and debris dumpsters that had yet to be removed. She went down her morning mental checklist as she maneuvered out of the neighborhood. She had put a stamped envelope in the mailbox as she backed out of the driveway. *Dinner is planned—but did I turn off the flat iron?*

Just as she turned off Meadowbrook, she saw their neighbors around the corner, Bob and Liz Winters, having a commotion in front of their house. Their dogs were barking and raising Cain through the glass storm door. The police and the Suits were there. With a rough hand on his head, Bob was already being shoved in the squad car, still in his undershirt. She was being handcuffed, face down on the hood. For a brief moment, they made eye contact. The blonde woman slightly shook her head "no" as if to warn her not to acknowledge her—just keep driving. Jude immediately averted her eyes and turned the corner, horrified at what she had just witnessed.

Poor Liz is still in her bathrobe and missing one slipper. What in the world could that be about? They had been friends for years. He was an engineer, and she was a 5th grade math teacher. They had brought in one of the casseroles to Grayson's memorial lunch just last year. Just ordinary people. *Why were they being arrested?*

She hit the earpiece and instructed it to call home. Jackson answered on the second ring. "Did you leave your flat iron on again?" he asked.

"No, worse," said Jude. "The Winters have just been arrested!"

"Are you serious!? Are you sure?" he asked in disbelief.

"He was in the squad car, and she was being handcuffed," Jude replied. "Please don't leave the house today, son. It's getting too dangerous."

"Agreed," he said. "I hope this isn't all for nothing, Mom. I hope I haven't added to your stress level by staying off that stupid census."

"Don't second-guess it now," she replied. "I think there may come a time when we'll be thankful we made that decision."

"Be careful, Mother."

"All right. Check on Jessica. She's sleeping in this morning, I guess. I'll call you if I see anything else strange on my way in. See you tonight. And Jackson?"

"Yes, Mom?"

"Go ahead and check that flat iron."

As Jude was putting on her lab coat, she looked at Daniel and Spencer already hard at work. It had started to feel like they were all part of a hodgepodge family. War does that to people; they live in the moment. They never know what tomorrow holds, so for today, they are going to live it to the fullest.

They had formed a close bond. She was even helping them on the secret project for the C-Camp prisoners. They had constructed a casket with a secret compartment in the bottom of it so it could actually hold two bodies. It wasn't perfected yet, but close.

Spencer was in charge of the actual daily casketing with his youthful strength and muscular build. He was easily able to handle the job alone or with the use of one of the 20-foot, remote controlled body lifts. He had gone to the Camps so much over the last few weeks, it was nothing for him to wrap and lift a 250 lb. man on his own and place him in the removal casket for transport. Cumbersome, but he could handle it. At the funeral home, he tried to always use the lift on the men and heavier women. The straps went under the shoulders, hips and calves. Then he hit the remote, and up they went. Roll the casket underneath and lower them gently down. It saved his back. Daniel and Jude dressed and customized them. It was heartbreaking the number of people being brought in from the Camps along with the soldiers from their area. It seemed so unreal.

Today, Jude had recognized a lady from her church and also a young man who had graduated from high school with Jackson. They were both Camp casualties. It was hitting close to home now. She couldn't help but wonder if she, Jackson or Jessica would be taken there. Their church was one of the ones that had disbanded. Nobody wanted to be imprisoned for a Sunday morning communion.

Early on in their relationship, Jude had just openly asked Daniel where they stood related to their beliefs. At first, he and Spencer had both gotten quiet and looked around to see who all was in the prep room. "Shhhhhh," Daniel had cautioned putting his finger up to his lips.

"Why the secrecy? We're alone, aren't we?" Jude had whispered.

"There are things going on in the business world we've been forbidden to discuss with employees, even at the funerals, which is odd. But since technically you're not an employee, you're contract, I'll fill you in. We have to be careful to see where Lucy is. She's not a Believer, and from what I've learned from outside sources, her family is heavily involved with the Black Suit Order. You know—the 'Suits'?"

"Oh, my." Jude shuddered, quickly replaying in her mind the few conversations she had actually had with Lucy over the years, wondering if she had ever witnessed to her. For the first time in her life, she was hoping she hadn't. Jude had shared the story of the bombing with Daniel and Spencer way back when and how the Suits had overrun the courthouse in Dallas when Lamar Street was bombed. That's how they had all begun being open with each other about their beliefs, and when she had confided about Lucy having the same last name as Jessica's husband, Spencer had looked up shocked from his struggling to get a strap under a 400 lb. man.

"Seriously? Straps is married?" Spencer had asked.

"Straps?" Jude said.

"Who in the world is Straps?" Daniel asked.

Spencer looked a little embarrassed. "That's what I call Jessica sometimes. She's always saying she has a 40 lb. kid strapped to her waist, so I started calling her Straps."

Daniel was sorry he had asked. He hoped Jude wasn't offended. "I'll bet she just loves that," Jude said sarcastically, chuckling under her breath with one finely arched eyebrow raised. Daniel was relieved that she thought it was as funny as he did. They had gotten to know Jessica and her dry humor. It made them both laugh out loud to think about him calling her Straps. They were all spending more and more time together and were relaxed in each other's company.

Chapter 19

Making Plans

Today, the guys were already working on the C-Project in between prepping bodies. Daniel, with his sleeves rolled up, watched her as she walked up. He never wore the lab coats. She had never asked him why, it was just an observation. This morning, she could tell he had something on his mind.

"Come with us," Daniel said to her quietly, and she immediately followed. They took her into the cooler where they stored the bodies. There was something they wanted to show her which required them to lock the prep room door from the inside before they did. They led her to "the secret."

Spencer looked over at his dad. "It's time we show her." Daniel nodded, and so they did. They had a false door which led to an underground tunnel that went straight to Daniel's private mausoleum. It was huge and empty. "We figure it'll come in handy once we start to make the rescues—like a holding place, between point A to point B. We are as certain as you guys are that this is the beginning of the end. Every morning, we wake up wondering what's happened while we slept—and if we're still free."

Jude, still staring up at him, replied, "We need to bring Jessica and Jackson in on this. Are you guys coming for dinner again tomorrow night?" she asked. "I really want you to tell Jackson about this." They had been having dinner with them once a week since the earthquake. "Say 7:00, like always? I'm just making curry chicken and potatoes, nothing fancy. The grocery stores no longer get the deliveries they used to so we just get what's available. I'm down to my last pack of chops that I'm making tonight, but I still have a few random selections."

Spencer was quick to respond. "Sounds great to us." He accepted the invitation for both of them without so much as a glance at Daniel. "Don't get me wrong now," Spencer said, looking at his dad, "I love chocolate chip pancakes, but chicken—actual meat every week. It's been great!"

They both exchanged happy glances at the thought of a chicken dinner prepared by neither one of them. Jude smiled at their enthusiasm. She had fallen for Daniel—hook, line and sinker. There was definitely strong chemistry between them. They both had agreed they wanted to get to know each other better, and they had. The weekly dinners had provided the catalyst to do just that. Outside dating seemed something of the past. All the movie theaters had closed down except one. Wartime creates a different environment, especially with the government lording over your every move. It was nice to just meet at her house and everybody feel at ease. Jackson and Spencer could chat for hours. Spencer and Jessica had hit it off easy, too. She pretended all the names he hung on her made her mad. But she actually enjoyed the back and forth banters.

"Then it's settled," Jude said. "There may even be a pot roast in your near future. I think I spied one in the deep freeze this morning." She winked at him.

He threw his arms up and lifted his head up to the heavens! "Ahhhhhhhh," he said in mock praise. Daniel and Jude just shook their heads. He acted as though he hadn't eaten meat in a month, and she knew better as she had cooked hamburgers and homemade fries last week for them all. He had eaten two, Jackson three. It was nice that among the death, grief and chaos, they could still enjoy some lighthearted conversations along with some family meals.

All of a sudden, a big clap of what sounded like thunder shook and rattled the building, snapping them out of their jovial conversation. So they showed her how the door in the cooler took them to another door which led to the tunnel to Daniel's mausoleum.

After Daniel gave her a quick 101 on procedures and protocol should they need to utilize the secret passageway, they all went back to work. Before long, morning had given way to a lunchtime pepperoni pizza eaten off paper plates and served with ice cold soda cans stuck in black koozies. By the six o'clock hour, they had the last "dearly departed" casketed and moved into the Chapel and were ready to scrub out. Daniel washed his hands with the surgical soap and smiled, thinking of the meal they would share tomorrow night. He was head over heels for Jude and her family although he still kept a respectful distance. Death of a spouse and timing was a delicate matter. He wanted to approach with caution. He hadn't even tried to hold her hand or steal a kiss—not yet. He didn't want to ruin what they had started by acting like an eager 16 year old. But he knew already that he wanted to share everything with her.

"DAD!" Spencer pulled him back into the land of the living. Daniel jumped and chuckled at himself.

"I must have been daydreaming or something," he quickly rationalized.

"Let's get out of here," said Spencer, as he slung his suit coat over his shoulder and Jude grabbed her purse. Daniel watched her as she walked to her car. "Uhhh, Dad? You going to lock up or just stare at Jude until she's out of the parking lot?" Spencer asked, making a big, exaggerated, sweeping motion with his hand.

Daniel turned to look at Spencer. "I'll remember that next time you're trying to make sure you're seated at the dinner table next to—what did you call her? Oh, Straps!"

They both laughed as they locked the doors of the funeral home. *"What a couple of characters we are,"* Daniel thought. *"Me, after a woman whose husband's clothes still hang in her closets, and Spencer making eyes at someone whose husband abandoned her in 'the family way.' They could really pick 'em."*

"Be careful driving home, Jude," shouted Spencer, as he jumped on his bike and put on his helmet. Before she could respond, they felt a huge rumbling. *Was it another earthquake?*

Jude froze for a moment as Daniel shouted from two cars over: "Bombing! And it's getting closer!"

"Wow!" Jude said. The rumbling stopped as soon as it started. "This is crazy." She stood very still, clutching the door handle, but everything seemed fine.

"It's okay now. Be careful going home. I'll check on you later!" he said. "See you tomorrow evening?"

"Yes," she said, as she fumbled with her things. "Remember, I'm not coming in tomorrow," she reminded him.

"Oh, I haven't forgotten," said Daniel. (How could he? He thought about her constantly. He could tell by her face she was rattled over the rumbling noise. He wished he could just take her home and make her feel safe.)

Chapter 20

Laugh It Up

Jude got into the car and headed home, hitting her car phone and instructing it to call Jessica. "Mother!" she answered on the first ring, "I was just about to call you. The bombs! I can hear a rumbling. It sounds like it's getting closer and closer to us!"

"It is," said Jude, still shaken. "I just can't imagine that it's made its way to Colleyville."

"Well," said Jessica, "we couldn't imagine an earthquake here either, but we can't say that anymore. Anyway, do you want to hear what Dr. White said today?"

"I sure do," said Jude. "I didn't forget. What did she say? What's all the back pain about?"

"Well, the main thing we talked about were the contractions I've been having regularly."

"You WHAT?! Contractions?" Jude sputtered. "Why haven't you told me before now? What's going on? What does this mean? Isn't it too early to be having them? Are they just Braxton Hicks?"

"Mother, hold on. I was going to tell you guys tonight, but I'll go ahead and tell you now if you'll let me actually speak. I'm dilated to a two," she said. "Looks like he will most likely come early."

"Well ..." Jude interrupted.

"Wait, Mother, let me finish. The strange thing is, she acted really funny towards me today—Dr. White. I can't put my finger on it, but something was, you know, off."

Jude was suspicious right away. "What?" said Jude becoming irritated. "Are you sure? What makes you think that? What did she do?"

"Well, like I said—it's—I don't know. She was just, different. As if I was a stranger. Like I hadn't been coming to her since you took me for my first 'woman doctor thingy' at 16. It made me very, very uncomfortable."

"It's called a Pap Smear, Jessica. Good grief."

"Whatever, Mom. She gave me the creeps today like she was on a cast call for the nursemaid in *The Omen*."

"Where are you, now?" asked Jude, concerned.

"Oh, I'm home. I'm on the back porch having some cantaloupe."

Dr. White went straight to her office the minute Jessica left and hit redial on her cell. "Tony," she said, "it could be any day. She's already beginning to dilate. You should step up your game if you want the plan to fall into place."

Tony's heart raced at hearing the news. *"It won't be long now,"* he thought, cracking his knuckles while listening to the doctor go on and on about things he could care less about. He had heard all he needed to hear. Jessica was about to pop that kid out. And when she did, he'd be close by to execute his plan. He finally hung up after an eternity of listening to her blather on about ruptured membranes and blood and mucus plugs and a bunch of other stuff that nearly made him vomit. He called his A-team and gave them updated instructions.

An hour later, he inched up a little closer to their house on Meadowbrook. This would be a nice page the Mitlows could hang on their refrigerator. From where he was sitting, he could just about see the big stainless steel double doors through the dining room window with the aid of his high-powered binoculars. He couldn't wait to see their faces, speechless for once in their lives at what he had planned. They were all soft in the head about each other. Imagine how they'll act when there is a milk guzzler thrown into the mix. He couldn't have come back to the States at a better time!

He took a long draw off a cigarette and stomped it into the vinyl floor mat inside the smoke-filled van. He laughed as he put the earphones back on and strained to hear Jessica's voice as she sat on the back porch talking to her mom. He could hear everything on the outside of the house—and wait a minute—was that Jackson he saw moving in front of the window? He shifted so fast he got his foot caught in the wires and jerked the earphones right out of his ears! He let out a string of curse words as his face slammed into the window. Thank goodness they were tinted!

He got back in place and took a deep breath. Now he could see him. He knew it! He knew he'd come running to momma's rescue. This was gonna be sweet! He couldn't wait. He called the headquarters right outside of Colleyville. It was located farther north, right down Hwy 26, just before entering into the Southlake area. It was Camp 2. They had just brought two people in from that same neighborhood this morning, thanks to his surveillance crew. "Close little community," he chuckled. "Wonder how close they'd be after hearing each other go in and out of questioning from the interrogation room. After a while, they all sing like canaries."

"Captain!" he said into the phone. "I've located another census dodger. Jackson Mitlow," he spat out.

"Are you sure?" said the Captain. "I don't want you to tip them off if it isn't a positive sighting."

"Oh, no. It's him," he guffawed. "I could see him through the window, someone big. It has to be him. Please set up a raid, or a questioning. I want him caught and out of the way! And don't send two or three Suits. You'd better send a dozen or more! You'll need them to take *him* down."

"Are you going to participate?" the Captain asked.

"NO!" he shouted, a shower of spit fanning out of his mouth. "It'd ruin the rest of my plan. But I'll be watching from the van. And thanks, Captain. You know this one's personal for me."

"No problem, Tony. Glad we can help."

"Well," Jessica said, still on the phone with her mom, talking with a mouthful of cantaloupe, "I think I really like Spencer."

"You're still married," Jude responded quickly.

"I wouldn't exactly call it a marriage anymore, Mom, nor was I planning on proposing. I was just making a statement."

Jude thought to herself, but didn't say it out loud: *Look here, kid, we're not trying to make a love connection. What with you being 62 months pregnant with another man's baby and all. But hey, whatever.*

Jessica started back in. "I'm happy about you and Daniel. I miss Dad as much as anybody, but it's nice to see a light in your eyes, especially with the way everything is nowadays. Now Jackson, that's another story." They both chuckled.

"He's fine now. He was just a little apprehensive at first. You let me handle Jackson," Jude said. "Daniel and I have chemistry, and we're both willing to see where it leads."

"Uhhhh, okay, Mom," Jessica interrupted, bringing the conversation to a screeching halt. "You and your chemistry need to talk to Jackson. Like tonight."

"Well, okay," Jude said, feeling silly. "Whatever. I better get off the phone anyway so I can pay attention to the road."

"Well, well, well," Tony said aloud to himself from the van, "both the little so and so's, I see. And thanks for confirming Jackson's whereabouts for me. I'll be seeing you all soon enough!"

After their pork chop dinner, Jessica gave Jude the "eye"—the "better-talk-to-Jackson-about-Daniel" eye. She took the hint as Jessica slipped out with a sly grin on her face.

"Jackson?" she asked, "may we have a quick word? I wanted to mention something to you without your sister being around."

"Okay, Mom, what's up?"

"She had her doctor's appointment today, and she is already dilated to a two," she said, as she got up and got the bowl of the thawed blackberries and poured cream over them. He was familiar with all things "woman" as he had a slew of them as customers. He knew all their girl talk simply from osmosis, not to mention growing up with Jessica who kept nothing private and would bellow just about anything through the bathroom door.

"Seriously?" he asked. "Is everything okay with the baby?"

"Yes, everything is okay with the baby. I think living under all this stress, pre-term delivery is fairly common."

"Well, what can I do besides keep an eye on her?" he asked.

"That's about it, but we need to be prepared just in case we have an emergency, like if we need to get to the hospital in the middle of the night or something. You're off the radar, so I'm the only one who can leave the house with her during curfew."

"Okay, I understand what you're saying. I'll make sure the cars are always gassed up and ready and the driveway is clear at night. I'll keep my eyes open. That it?" he said, standing up.

"Grab the berries and let's hit the couch for the news." Then she laid her hand on his and said, "Well, there is one more thing."

"Yeah? Why all the mystery? You're acting funny, Mom. What's going on?" he questioned, as he sat back down.

"Well, you know I love your dad very much, don't you?"

"Of course, Mom." His brows furrowed. "Come on, just spit it out. You can tell me anything."

"It's Daniel," she blurted out. "I'm starting to have real feelings for him. I don't know what's going to happen between us, if anything, but just out of courtesy, I wanted to just put it out there." He slipped his hand out from under hers and put his on top.

"Well, Mom, when I first saw you two together, it felt odd. I'm just telling it straight," he said. "You know, because of Dad and all, but hey, we live in this world, and you're still alive and beautiful. And besides all of that, I already knew, and I understand. I'd have to be blind not to see the way he looks at you. I appreciate you giving me the chance to put in my two cents, but I'm fine; I like the guy." She smiled at him. "It's all cool, Mom," he said, as he stood up again, pulling her up by the hand. "I know, I'm great," he said, raising both arms and flexing his muscles.

"And so humble," she added. "They'll be over for dinner tomorrow night," she reminded him.

"Sounds good," said Jackson, as he sauntered out of the dining room and into the den.

Jessica burst into peels of hand-muffled laughter as he came in the den. "Well, did y'all talk about Mom's 'chemistry'?" He contorted his face in the universal "something stinks," shook his head and sat down.

"Gross, now move your feet, perv. I don't want to catch that swelling in those 'cankles.'" She kicked at him as he sat down, and they both shook with silent laughter.

"Laugh it up, you two," Tony thought, as he watched through the window. He didn't know what they were laughing at since he couldn't get any signals from inside the house, but they wouldn't be for long. He wondered how funny it would be once they took Jackson out of the equation.

Chapter 21

The Car Wash

Jude enjoyed sleeping with no alarm clock waking her up. She loved waking up slowly, naturally, not rushed. Stretching and soaking up the morning, she noticed a beautiful redbird in the tall oak tree right outside her bedroom window. She didn't move; she just lay there and watched him. It had been so long since she had seen one, she wanted to enjoy the moment. She listened to him sing his beautiful song, preen his bright red feathers, then watched as he flew away.

She put on her long robe and slowly made her way downstairs to the coffee. She sipped the hot brew while she made her list of things to do to prepare for dinner tonight. She was looking forward to Daniel and Spencer coming—they all were. Jessica came downstairs, and Jude made them both toast and honey. Then she went to get a quick shower. After slathering on a spicy scented lotion, she rummaged through the closet and settled on a pair of skinny jeans and a thin, black scoop neck, summer sweater. She slipped on black flip flops and headed to the laundry room. After tossing the towels in the dryer, she punched in the code to disarm the alarm system and opened the garage door.

She let her hair hang loose today; she wouldn't be gone long. Grayson used to always fuss at the buns and clips. He'd asked her on more than one occasion, "What's the point of all that beautiful, long hair if you're only going to put it up every day?" She wished for a moment she had left it down more for him. And then her mind immediately went to Daniel. She flipped her hair back with her hand, got in the car and drove to the market.

Although these were perilous times, she still looked forward to preparing meals for all of them. Early in the day was the perfect time to go to the grocery store. The aisles were still clean and organized before the rush of mini-van moms with their broods who came in to shop while their little ones wailed for candy from the metal buggies. The shelves were sparse with the cities in such disrepair nationwide. It had definitely impeded delivery trucks. If your beef was coming from Wyoming, you were out of luck. It might be stuck on the trains for weeks. With her meager selection of staples and fresh chicken (she hoped it was fresh), she self-checked, slid her card through the reader and headed for the car.

While meandering through the earthquake-riddled streets, she stopped by the Church Street Car Wash to have the dust rinsed off. As she was lining up her tires, she noticed some of the Black Suit guys installing something electronic just above the wash bay. She didn't understand how those Black Suits never seemed to get dirty with all the jobs they appeared to be doing, such as being on a 20-foot ladder at a car wash. *What the heck?* She didn't know what they were doing up there, nor did she know what kind of device they were installing. She only knew she wanted no part of it. She immediately put her car in reverse and tried to back out, but it was too late. There were already two cars lined up behind her and neither showed any intention of moving.

She had noticed people had become more and more calloused with little or no regard for each other. It wasn't like TV portrayed it, when after the crisis, the community comes together waving little candles, holding hands and singing "Kumbaya." It was just the opposite—every man for himself. "Plow over anybody who gets in your way," seemed to be the new fad. People were discourteous, downright rude.

Jude didn't like the way the Black Suits seemed to have singled her out from their lofty perch and sneered as they saw her body language as she changed her mind regarding the car wash. Too late, her car was committed. It was already on the track being moved forward. Her heart pounded as the wheels began to turn. The young attendant motioned for her to shift to neutral with hand signals. She had no choice at this point. She was being ogled by the prying eyes of the Suits as her car rolled underneath them through the wash entrance.

About halfway through the cycle, the whole thing lurched to a halt. Shrill groaning and screeching sounds along with the drip, drip, drip of the water surrounded her. Jude didn't panic at first, but she instinctively hit the automatic locks. She sat there. Nothing. She couldn't see through the streams of soapy water. It was dark. She felt something bump into her car. That did it. Her instincts kicked in full force. She slipped her .38 out of the glove box and laid it across her lap. She could shoot straight at close range. She had never pulled her gun, but this was indeed a special circumstance. She was trapped! Only the Suits knew she was in there. Her car was covered in the pink washing bubbles. She was unable to make out any of her surroundings—not even if there was a car in front of her! Her hand felt damp on the smooth black handle. It was quiet except for the faint sound of 1970's car wash music along with the drip, drip, drip of the water.

She flipped the wipers on and caught sight of a scruffy man with a shaggy beard approaching the front of her car. He came close enough to fog the window. He looked hideous, with yellowed, staggered teeth. He was yelling through the windshield, "Roll down your window!" He moved towards her, water and bubbles dripping down his face and clothes.

Jude's heart was pumping wildly as she tightened her grip on the handle of the revolver in her lap. "Who are you kidding?!" she shouted. "Are you insane?"

"I'm not going to hurtcha lady," came the muffled street slang through the soap. He wiped his mouth and put his face right up against the window glass. "Just wanted to talk a minute 'bout the car wash problem," he said, as he placed both palms on the window with a near toothless grin, every breath re-fogging the window.

"Move away from my car!" she demanded through gritted teeth. Her finger now moved on to the trigger. He tried the handle, and Jude raised the pistol and aimed it right at him. His eyes widened, and he turned and ran, disappearing into the pale blue squeegee strips. The wash cranked back up like a slow moving machine, restarting the rinse cycle. Her car was propelled the rest of the way down the tire tracking, while the eerie sound of the 70's music got louder and louder as she neared the exit.

As soon as the blinking red light turned green, and the manikin urged all patrons to shift into "D" and move forward, Jude gladly put her car in gear and took off away from the frightening car wash. The Suits stared after her, laughing as she sped away. Once safely down the street, the Suits slipped the homeless man a $20 bill and a towel. Her heart didn't stop pounding until she turned on her street.

Still shaking, she pulled into the garage and closed it, not noticing the black cars parked in front of her house. When she walked in, Jackson, standing in his black gym shorts and shirtless was cracking the seal on a bottle of water. He took one look at her face and said, "What's wrong, Mother? Something happen at the store?" He put the water down and put his hand on her shoulder.

"No," she replied, "the car wash." Still breathless, she told him of the Suits outside of the car wash and then the homeless man inside the wash, like he knew it was going to jam at just that moment. How he had tried the door handle, and she had showed him her gun. She relived the whole episode. Jude was terrified at the possibilities if he had gotten in her car. Jackson fumed, stomping and snorting around just at the thought of somebody scaring her like that! Jude insisted that he not go down to the car wash. It wasn't worth getting off the radar for. No real harm had been done. They both calmed down and agreed that the Suits coupled with the homeless man was not a coincidence; it was deliberate.

Chapter 22

Surrounded

The door bell sounded, and Jude jumped. They both looked at each other. "Daniel's not supposed to be here until late this evening. Who could that be?" Jude questioned.

"It's the Suits," Jessica whispered, as she ran into the kitchen where they were. I looked out the peep hole. "There's a whole group of them!"

Jude panicking, shouted quietly, "Run upstairs, Jackson! Jackson!" she begged, pushing him. "Just go upstairs, and get in the attic! Let me take care of this! We don't even know why they're here," she pleaded. She tried to shove him toward the stairs, but he wouldn't budge.

"WAIT! Okay, Mother," he finally ground out between clenched teeth, "but I hate it! Hiding while you two ...." his voice trailed off as he took the stairs two at a time. He turned one final time at the top of the stairs with outstretched arms. "I swear, if they lay a hand on either one of you, I'll kill them all!"

Jude took a deep breath and opened the door. Jessica ran back to the couch and propped her feet up, trying not to look staged. "May I help you?" Jude said, in a strained cheerful voice.

"Maybe," said one of the four guys in the Suits and dark glasses. "May we come in?"

"Well," Jude stammered, "my daughter really isn't feeling well. Could you maybe ...." The heavyset Suit had already put a heavy black boot in the door.

"It'll just take a minute, ma'am," he said, as they all pushed past her, looking around.

"Okay, what is all this?" she asked, trying to sound brave and authoritative while she watched them scatter like roaches through the den and kitchen.

"We got a couple of questions for you, Ms. Mitlow."

"Okay," she said, as they looked past her, glancing up the staircase.

"You seem a little nervous, Ms. Mitlow. Now why would that be?" one of the Suits smirked, while talking to the back of her head. Jude jerked when she felt him behind her and turned around quickly.

"How many people are living in this house?" another asked, so close to her face she could smell the stale cigarette smoke on his breath.

"Two." The lie slid easily off her tongue.

"Just two, Ms. Mitlow?" the third Suit chimed in, as he took the first few stairs in a taunting manner. Four more Suits came in the front door without so much as a knock.

"Yes, just my daughter and I," she said, looking around from Suit to Suit, desperately wanting to steer them away from the stairs. "And don't you need a search warrant to go through my house?"

"Now why would we need a search warrant? You got something to hide?" Some gathered around her while others went up to the second floor. "Where is your son, Ms. Mitlow? We have no record of his census report and no current living address. Now we find that odd, Ms. Mitlow, and highly illegal."

"Come out, come out, wherever you are, Jackson," bellowed the Suit climbing the stairs. Jude looked right at the heavy Suit.

"I told you I haven't seen him. He travels a lot in his business."

"He travels a lot in the FITness business?" he asked, shaking his large head up and down holding up his fingers in the quotations signs. "That doesn't sound very realistic, Ms. Mitlow."

Jude was trying to keep up with whoever was asking the question as they began to circle around her. She spun from one to the other, around and around as they grilled her, hair swinging wildly. "We think you know where he is, and we think you're not wanting to tell us. Now we can understand that," he said with a sarcastic sympathy nod pooching out his thick lips. "Now, you take Charlie over there," he wagged his heavy head. "He's got a couple of kids, don't you Charlie?" One of the Suits grunted in response. "We aren't going to DO anything to him, we just need an accurate count in each subdivision so we can protect you." They smiled at one another.

"Hiding him or deceiving us intentionally, well, that wouldn't bode well for any of you. Might even lead to your arrest—and your daughter. Now, you wouldn't want that baby to be born in jail, would you, Jude?" he asked, as he looked directly behind her. Jude turned to see Jessica standing in the doorway holding a bat. "And what are you planning on doing with that bat, little lady?"

"Oh, I don't know. I was thinking about batting a few 'balls' around, sir." They all chuckled. He held his arms out wide in mock surrender, showing his midsection bulging over his suit pants.

"Brave. I'll give you that. You really wanna take a swing at me? I'd say you're pretty much outnumbered."

"You have no idea," Jessica thought to herself, knowing Jackson was listening and/or watching. And he was. He squinted his eyes through the darkness of the attic and licked his lips. A drop of sweat rolled down his forehead. He barely noticed. He had both eyes trained on the scene below.

The rest of the Suits filed back down the stairs. They appeared to have guessed he wasn't there or he was hiding really well.

"Come on, J.W., let's go. He ain't here. He'd have already rushed out to save his momma."

"Well, hon," the big one said to Jessica, "it's against the law to not report every family member who's living in each residence. Now, I don't make the laws, but I do enforce them. We know you're a lawyer. We haven't crossed any lines here today."

Jude immediately stepped in front of Jessica. "Okay, that's enough! Get away from her. You've searched the house. I told you, he's not here. You satisfied?" she said, starting to get angry and walking to the front door.

"Well, it'd be a shame to lose all that pretty black hair," the heavy one said, reaching out to feel a thick lock. Jude jerked it out of his pudgy hand, but it had gotten tangled in an ornament that hung from a gold chain he was wearing. Jude wrenched her hair free of what looked like a golden snake or cobra.

"What are you talking about? Are you threatening me? You're going to cut my head off over a census report?" Jude said, with her voice rising.

"NO, ma'am. I did not say that at all. You must have misunderstood me, Jude. We don't cut ANYbody's head off," he said, as all the Suits gathered in the foyer. "We're not ISIS. All I'm saying is, if we find out he's here and you were lying to us, you could be arrested. When you go to them Camps," he drawled out, "first thang they do? Buzz that head. Kind of equals things out ya know. High class broads ain't quite so high and mighty sportin' a crew cut!" They all chuckled and elbowed one another.

"Now that's about enough," Jude said. "If you're going to arrest me, then do it. If not, get out!"

Heavy raised his arms in mock surrender. "No need in you getting all riled up, ma'am. We're just doing our job. Let's go, boys!" They dramatically tipped their hats and single filed out the door. Jude noticed they were all wearing the same serpent chain. She clicked the dead bolt behind them and pressed her back up against it.

Her heart was pounding in her ears. They couldn't see Jackson, but he could see them through the air conditioner vent. He quietly crawled backwards and put the AR-15 back on its stand. He swung down from the attic stairs, and they snapped shut with a bang. Jessica backed up against the wall and let the bat sag and put one hand over her heart, breathing heavy as Jackson came down the stairs.

"We gotta do something, guys. I need to disappear. I don't want them coming back here."

"NO. Don't even think that," Jude said firmly, grabbing his shoulder. "We need you here. Just stay in the house. No more going to the store or the gym or late night motorcycle riding. Nothing. I would never rest again not knowing where you are. First thing tomorrow morning, Jessica and I will go close down the gym."

She reached up and brushed off insulation from one of his arms. A fine sheen of perspiration made it glisten like diamond dust. "We'll say you've moved out of state or something. But I think as long as you stay in the house we'll be okay."

"There is no use arguing with her," he thought *"she's right."* "All right, Mom, I'll do it for you, but I could go to Decatur to the hideout."

"No!" they both shouted at once. "Are you crazy?" Jessica said. "And leave us here?" By this time, they were nearly in tears.

"I just don't know what to do, guys. Do you know how bad I wanted to come through the ceiling and rip them apart, limb from limb?"

"I know, son, but we have to think ahead, keep our wits about us. We'll figure it out." She was the only one he listened to. And that was stretching it a bit.

"While they're investigating us or spying or whatever they call it," said Jackson, "we'll play it safe. I'll keep out of sight as long as they don't put their hands on you. But at that point, Mother, not even you can stop me," he said, as he subconsciously felt a lock of Jude's hair. "I'd never forgive myself if anything happened to either of you on my account."

Tony dialed the cell, and the Suit answered. "Well? Let's hear it. Did you give them a good scare?"

"Yeah. She was quaking in her boots. The 'knocked-up' one came in, too—feisty little broad."

"Yeah, whatever," Tony said, irritated. "Her day's coming, but did you see any evidence of him? That's what I care about today."

"I couldn't tell if he was there or not," answered the heavy. Tony slammed his fist down on the dash of the van.

"I lost sight of him some time last night, too. I figured using the women as bait would get him to expose himself. But I guess he went and hid under the bed." They both chortled. "I'll try and figure out where he goes. In the meantime, were you able to put the bug anywhere?"

"No, that witch followed our every move—a real she-cat."

"We've got time," Tony said, nursing his now-bruised hand. "Are you guys going to the convention?" Tony asked, fingering his chain with the golden serpent.

"Oh, yeah, looking forward to it. Supposed to be over a million strong, like Woodstock."

"Can't wait," said Tony. "And what about the President?"

"You know you're not supposed to talk about it on live air, Tony, but it's being 'handled.'"

"Oh, yeah, I gotcha. Just getting anxious. All these Bible thumpers will be contained once and for all. The fools really think the census is about population. Sheep to the slaughter, while we're making room for the real King." They both immediately held the number one sign in the middle of their foreheads and pressed the ornament held by the chain up to their lips and kissed it. "Long live the King," they both said dutifully in unison.

They all caught their breaths, relieved the Suits had finally left. Jessica reached down and felt her bulging belly. "It nearly kicked a hole through my stomach when that creep got too close to me."

"Well, 'it' needs a name," said Jude.

"Yeah, I know, but I haven't decided yet," replied Jessica. "I'll know when I see him which one fits the best.

"Okay," said Jackson, putting both arms up in surrender, "let's name the baby later, like *AFTER* we get all the guns out of Dad's safe so we can actually protect 'it' and ourselves."

They opened the door to Grayson's study, something they didn't do often now. Jude had said it felt empty and quiet. It was cool and dark with the richer woods and heavy drapes. There were globes on golden spinners, two overstuffed chairs for reading and a beautiful picture of Jude in her wedding dress. The familiar green banker's lamp was on Grayson's desk. There were framed high school pictures of both kids on the wall as well as a family snapshot of their favorite trip to Cabo San Lucas. They waxed nostalgic for a brief moment as they stepped in. Jude pulled up the drapes in one big swoop and tiny particles of dust floated and danced in the sunbeams. Bookcases filled with years of collecting books on various subjects and several Bibles in all shapes and translations lined the shelves.

Jackson removed an old, hardback copy of *Moby Dick* and pressed on a panel. It exposed a combination lock. "One to the right, two to the left, one to the right, in case y'all have forgotten," said Jackson, as he twisted the knob. "It's Mom's birthday."

"I remember," said Jessica.

It opened up, and they started removing the long hunting rifles and a couple of shotguns, assembly-line fashion, until it was empty.

"There's something else I've been working on, too," said Jackson. There wasn't time to tell you earlier during the commotion, but come into the dining room.

They all filed out of Grayson's office. Jude took her time turning off the lights and closing the drapes. She let her eyes linger on his favorite spot where he read every evening for years. She missed him so much. All still on emotional overload and each carrying weapons, they walked into the dining room and Jackson stopped.

"Put the guns down. Remember where the earthquake loosened up all of these wooden slats? Well, right below here," Jackson tapped his foot, "Daniel and I used a portion of the house that was intentionally left hollow for utility service and cleared it out. It was designed for plumbing or electrical emergency access." He raised a hinged opening. "We can put the weapons in here to be able to get to them quicker."

"It looks like a casket," commented Jessica.

"Well, it is one, but it's perfect for hiding weapons and even one of us if it came down to it," replied Jackson.

They finished putting the guns in and clicked it shut and headed toward the kitchen. Jessica glanced back toward the tomb and a shiver ran down her spine. Jude put the tea kettle on. Seems like there is nothing a cup of hot tea can't soothe. They were still coming down from the emotional rollercoaster the Suits had brought.

They sat down and began to tally up all of the strange events over the last few months, trying to gain some perspective. Jackson had noticed several weeks ago when he'd gone to their church in Bedford to help the pastor close the church by order of the City Council, that the traffic lights were all making strange, alien-type sounds. "I think it's all part of that tracking system."

Jude shook her head as she sipped the hot tea. "I thought those signal sounds were for the blind."

"Really, Mother? How many blind people have you seen at the corner of Central Drive and Bedford Road? Think about it; they may be under the pretense of 'for the blind,' but I'm not buying it—any of it."

"I'm glad you left your SUV at the funeral home," Jude said randomly. Both kids looked up at each other.

"Yeah, and I'm not going back for it. Not now. I have a feeling I'll never be driving it again."

"Oh, don't say that, baby doll," said Jude.

"And don't get sentimental now, Mom, and start using my baby names. We have to face some hard realities here." Jude put on her brave face and nodded in agreement.

"I nearly went postal on that one old dude, the heavy one. I would have loved to have cracked his head open," said Jessica. "The only thing that stopped me is, I knew you'd have to come finish the job—I mean mob—I mean blob!" They both laughed. Jude glared over at them.

"Too soon to joke, Mom?" Jackson asked. "We're sorry." He glanced at Jessica, and they stopped.

Jackson headed upstairs, and Jude wordlessly began washing the chicken in the sink and preparing it to go in the oven. She covered it in salt, pepper and curry powder, then rubbed butter into every pore of its skin as her mind drifted in and out on the day's events as Jessica watched. When she started filling the cavity with onions and garlic cloves, Jessica piped up with, "Mom? Would you like to be left alone with that bird?"

Jude pursed her lips and shook her head. "Really, Jessica!"

She pulled out a sheet of foil and wrapped the clear baking dish and put it in the oven, then announced she was headed up the stairs to relax a while. She wasn't ready to joke or make light of anything. Normally, they all handled stress with jokes, but not today. Today, she had really felt threatened. She'd had all she could take for one afternoon. *The car wash, the Suits, Jackson being actively sought after, what was next?*

Jude sank down into a luxurious tub filled with steaming hot water and vanilla bath salts. A half a dozen apple-scented candles lined the countertop and tub. The mirrors were completely fogged over. She loved her hot baths.

Jude had called Daniel right before she stepped in and had told him what had happened. He hated that he wasn't there or able to protect her. He knew Jackson could handle it fine, but he cared for her and wanted to be the one she depended on. He wasn't used to being the guy on the phone; he was used to being the guy with the gun. He was grateful for Jackson's patience. Had he been there, he told her, he may have lost his cool and been the one receiving a crew cut this evening.

She had soaked away the Suits and tried to put it all behind her. She languished in the tub for nearly an hour, then grabbed an oversized white towel and dried off. She strolled through her closet trying to choose the best outfit for the evening. She was so looking forward to Daniel coming over. She didn't want to overdress, but wasn't about to sport her yogas and T. She laughed at the thought: *"Welcome, y'all, come on in and get your pajamas on. That's what we wear every night around here unless we have company."* She chuckled as she slid on a pair of faded jeans and an expensive leopard print shirt with black fringe. She applied soft makeup and a tinted lip gloss and looked in the full-length mirror. She debated on leaving her hair up in the clip but decided a high ponytail would be perfect (not really up or down). She put on gold hoop earrings and grabbed a stack of gold bangle bracelets and slipped them on as she left the room barefoot. *"Oh, yeah,"* she thought, as she looked down and wiggled her toes, *"I guess I need to think about shoes. Gold strappy sandals."* "Yep," she said aloud, as she walked past her dressing mirror, "that'll do."

Chapter 23

Girl Functions and the Broken Cup

At 7:00 p.m. sharp, the doorbell rang. Jude quickly took off her apron and shoved it in the pantry on its hook. She went to the door and invited them both in, hoping she didn't smell like chicken. He lit up when he saw her—he always did. His hair looked rich and dark, nearly black. It had grown out a little and was combed straight back, damp and a little wavy from a recent shower. He did something he had never done before. He brushed a kiss on her cheek as he came in. It felt as natural as rain but still made her blush. He smelled wonderful up close. She loved his musky cologne.

"Come on in, you two," said Jude. She noticed they both had worn cool-looking designer jeans. Spencer must have brought him on board, like Jackson and Jessica had her, on all things stonewashed (if that was what they still did to jeans) and the latest fads. Spencer had on a tight T-shirt with a cross and a dove monogram. Daniel wore a white shirt, tail out and black sandals. He looked great.

Jessica stayed on the sofa, unable to help with the meal or even put ice in the glasses. Her hips felt heavy, and her back ached. She was still tuned up from the Suit inquisition earlier that afternoon. Jude had asked Jackson to serve the drinks instead. Spencer went in to keep Jessica company on the sofa while, reluctantly, Jackson served as "drink hostess" and got them all beverages. Daniel and Spencer both wanted sweet tea.

"Well, that's good," Jackson muttered to himself, "because I'm not about to put on an apron and start hand squeezing orange juice or anything. They can drink what we're drinking." He laughed at his own words. He'd just gone third grade on them, and they didn't even know it.

Jude invited Daniel into the kitchen, and they chatted while she put the finishing touches on the meal. He enjoyed watching her work in the kitchen—actually, he enjoyed any room she was in as long as he was there with her. He liked the way her ponytail swung when she would turn to answer his questions and the way she smiled at him. They both took the serving dishes to the dining room and called the kids in for dinner.

They gathered around the table, and Jude asked Daniel to say grace. He held his hands out and Jude and Spencer each took one. They all held hands while he prayed, not only for blessings over the meal, but also protection over each one of them in the days to come.

"Pass the bread," Jackson said, determined somebody was going to serve him something, too. Conversation flowed easily among them all. Jude looked around the table, content, and wondered how many more times a peaceful dinner would be had with the growing intensity of the government's intrusion. She had tried to go about their life; however, that was nearly impossible now. It seemed like every other day something heart-stopping was happening to her family. But tonight, they would enjoy and not take anything for granted.

After the delicious dinner of the promised curry chicken, potatoes and summer squash, Jude and Daniel began to clear the table while the boys helped Jessica back to the couch. Daniel asked Jude some personal questions regarding Jessica's "day." "I don't think she is in actual labor, but maybe at the beginning of her body making preparation. That happens a few days or weeks before the actual onset of labor," Daniel said, in "doctor mode."

Jude wholly agreed. "It's been many years since I delivered my babies, but I do remember those last few weeks. We've kept a close eye on her. It seems to come and go."

"She's got that 'walk'," Daniel added. Jude nodded in agreement.

They all ended up in the living room and began to talk about everything that was going on. Each one had something to add. Jude wanted Daniel to tell the rest of them about the funeral home tunnel. They took turns putting their stories out there. Jackson told of the suspect traffic signals, Spencer shared the events at the holding Camps and the casket they were modifying for a plan to rescue some of the prisoners.

"What we need is a system," Jude interjected. "We need somebody on the inside who could help organize and be part of the escape plan."

Spencer immediately agreed, but warned, "You can't trust the guards, but maybe later an opportunity will present itself."

Jessica told of the odd doctor's appointment. Jude also shared the car wash incident. They all agreed that it was getting close. To what, they didn't know, but it felt like the brink of something big to them all.

Daniel began to tell them about the secret tunnel that led to his personal mausoleum. "At first, we were just using the mausoleum as a way to store Bibles in case they were the next thing becoming outlawed. But then I thought, heck, think bigger! We still haven't worked out all of the details. Hopefully before too long, we can do a trial run with a volunteer willing to ride in the escape casket. It'll be hot and a snug fit, but necessary." Jude's eyes widened at the thought. It looked like Daniel and Spencer were both looking at her, mentally weighing her.

"Once we complete our first successful escape, they'll need to spend a few hours stashed away there making sure it's safe to come out. It can double as an escape route in case we're raided internally, too. I showed your mother today where the doors are."

"We have literally 'Shaw-shanked it,'" Spencer said, his look intense.

"Shaw what?" asked Jessica. "What in the world is shanking? I think Mom shanked the chicken before she put it in the oven."

"JESSICA!" Jude scolded. "Are you 10 years old?"

Jackson glanced at Spencer smiling, embarrassed, but it was hilarious! "It's from an old movie, Sis, where they dug or shanked out a tunnel from the prison."

"Okay, then, I get it. Sorry, Mom." Suddenly, Jessica interrupted herself with a contorted face and loud groan and grabbed her stomach. "Ohhhhhh … OOOOOOOOhhhhh … what the? GUYS! Mother!"

Jude rushed over to her. "Is it the baby?"

"Yes!" she said breathless. She tried to make light of it, but they could all see she was in real breathtaking pain. "I think he's actually trying to 'shank' his way out." Nobody laughed. They took a recess to see if the contractions were going to stop. Daniel timed them on his wrist watch. She lay on her side, feet in Spencer's lap and Jackson kneeling down beside her, rubbing her belly to try to soothe her. Jude wanted to boil water or something, but she didn't. She spoke softly to her. Daniel was at the ready; he could drive, or he could deliver. Either way he was ready to go.

Tony watched anxiously from the van. He was breathing hard with anticipation, his knee nervously bouncing up and down. Man, this might be it! He could see broken pieces of the scene through the small space in the blinds. He could make out that "shirtless wonder" he saw in the yard after the earthquake, and Jude, of course—the other man, he didn't know. Has to be that funeral home guy—the owner Lucy had informed him about. He'd have to watch out for those two. From here, he couldn't see if Jackson was there or not. He was probably still hiding under the bed. He chuckled at his own humor and turned up the outside bug to see if he could hear anything through the window. Nada. Not a word. But even with his lack of knowledge, all that attention they were giving Jessica—it had to be about the kid.

After about 20 minutes, the contractions all but dissipated. They all somewhat relaxed after confirming the baby wasn't trying to come at that moment. Jackson slouched back in his recliner. Daniel got up and stretched his back. *(Jude was ready to gently ask her to remove her jeans and let her do a visual inspection, to look to see if the baby was actually*

crowning, but decided to keep those thoughts to herself.) Luckily, Daniel had been involved in enough medical training while overseas that included OBGYN rotations, that he knew the right questions to ask her. He had delivered at least two dozen, maybe more. He remembered the signs well, and she was definitely getting close. He told them within the next two to five days they'd have a baby.

"Please don't ask me to hold anything besides her hands, if I'm here at the big moment," Spencer said nervously. "I mean, I think you guys are great and all, but I'm not good with this kind of stuff." He had zero experience, and he wasn't ready to gain any information on the delicate subject of girl functions outside of the normal areas of personal interest. Jackson teased him about helping out with the delivery, mentioning something about a trash bag, some rope and a pulley, and Spencer got up and escaped to the bathroom. They all laughed him all the way down the hall.

"Guys!" Jude admonished, but joined in the laughter. "Poor Spencer. We're really breaking you guys in good, Dan," she said, as she laughed. Daniel looked over at her, still chuckling from the heckling Spencer was getting. Nobody had ever called him Dan except his mother, and she had been gone for years. He loved the way his name sounded on her lips.

"Hey, Daniel," Jessica said, still recovering, "FYI, I don't know if Mom told you, but when I was five months along, they did a sonogram and told me it was a boy. Just so you know."

"That's great news, Jessica. Congratulations."

"Would you like for me to call your doctor or anything?" Daniel kindly offered.

"Absolutely not," said Jessica immediately. "She creeped me out so bad yesterday, I'm not sure anymore that I want her involved, at least I don't tonight. She treated me like a science project. I don't know how I'll feel when I get to the hospital when it's the real deal, but tonight? No, thank you."

"No problem," he said.

"You really need to be checked though, since you did have some dilation started." Spencer returned just in time to hear his dad make the last comment and watched him make some sort of awkward hand signal like he was picking up a dime with all of his fingers off of the coffee table.

"Is that some sort of code for something, Dad?"

"Trust me, Spence, you don't want to know."

The girls both laughed, and finally, the conversation drifted back to the funeral home and the mausoleum.

"We '*dug*' a tunnel," Daniel explained (emphasizing the word dug instead of shank), "from the basement, over to the mausoleum—about 80 feet out. So, besides it being pitch black all the way through, it's the perfect getaway."

"Not to sound morbid, but how did you dig in a cemetery without running into, uhhh, you know, so and so's granddaddy?" Jackson asked.

Jude just shook her head and closed her eyes, but he did have a point. Daniel and Spencer smiled at how it sounded. "Well, I took that into consideration when I drew up the plans, Jackson. Spencer did have a close call at one point (they both glanced at each other with an inappropriate smile), but we worked around it so to speak."

Jackson stood up and stretched his legs and told about their property with the underground living quarters. He told them about Decatur and of his and his dad's work out there. He suggested they go see it, and added, "It might be the perfect place to take the rescued people."

Jude spoke up. "We all sure have a lot of hideouts and dungeons. It sounds like a movie script."

Nothing about the last eight months seemed even remotely familiar. Her mind drifted to Bob and Liz, the neighbors she had witnessed being arrested. Jude wondered how they were making out at the Camp. Thankfully, she hadn't seen either one come through the funeral home during Spencer's pickups, so at least she could assume for now they were both still alive.

Jude naturally gravitated to where Jackson was standing, Jessica noticed, to see if he needed some more tea or anything. *"Oh, well,"* she thought, *"I didn't want Mom to baby me anymore tonight anyway."* She started thinking about how she and her mom had really gotten a lot closer since she had moved in, but it was still all mostly about Jackson—*"The Chosen One."* She laughed to herself about the momentary age-old jealousy. Jackson was innocent. He had never understood what she was referring to. And she figured at this point, it no longer mattered.

They finished the evening with coffee and pound cake. The boys stayed in the living room while Daniel helped Jude put away the dessert dishes. She loaded the dishwasher while they chatted, wanting to spend as much time together as they could.

Jackson came into the kitchen. "Hey, guys, we're going to go ahead and watch a DVR recording to get Jessica's mind off of everything. Do y'all want us to wait?"

"No," they both said at once.

Then Jude said, "You guys go ahead. We're going to go to the back patio with another cup of coffee and visit for a while." Daniel took both of their cups and headed out.

Jackson leaned over and whispered to her, "Why don't you leave all that chemistry in here, Mom?"

"Shh, stop that, Jackson, come on." She swatted at him. "You're embarrassing me, but, hey." She flipped her ponytail around. "I've still got it, so don't come peeking out the patio window." She left him standing jaw agape.

Jude and Daniel sat together on the porch swing listening to the crickets and sipping their coffee. He let his hand casually slip over to where her hand rested inches from his. Neither one jerked away but just let their hands touch, side to side. The pull was so strong between them,

Jude wondered if Daniel was feeling the same way she did. She didn't want to do anything inappropriate, but she really wanted to take their relationship to the next level. Her heart was beating a little faster, and the coffee seemed to be making her unusually warm. Or was it just the Texas heat affecting her?

Daniel was mentally talking himself through the next steps or wondering if there should be any. He would approach with some tactical maneuvering; come in at just the right angle. He needed to think this through. *"Should I actually put my hand over hers? Should I just tell her how I feel?"* He knew he wasn't reading her wrong. She hadn't pulled away when he touched her hand. *"What the heck; I'm going for it!"*

He had just leaned over to kiss her and was immediately aware that he should have taken two hot cups of coffee into account. Jude jumped up, grabbing her burning leg, trying to hold the wet fabric of her jeans away from her thigh, and in the meantime, dropped her cup and it shattered to the ground with enough noise to wake the dead. Daniel was grabbing for the cups as the hot liquid burned him! Mercifully, his cup stayed in his hand as he shouted, "Don't move! There's broken glass." She froze and raised both hands. He brushed the broken pieces over with his foot and that put him face to face with her.

He looked at her and said, "What I was trying to do, was this." And with his one free arm, he circled her waist and pulled her the final three inches to him—not too gentle, but abrupt. Forcefully, but not insulting. She felt like she was in a western movie. And when he was finished, she knew she'd been kissed.

The noise from the shattering glass had made the boys run to the patio door, but Jude and Daniel never heard it open. When they finally looked up, Spencer's mouth was slightly ajar and Jackson was grinning like the Grinch who stole Christmas.

Unfortunately, there was somebody else eavesdropping on the evening. He couldn't see into the screened-in portion of the patio. Tony, his forehead glistening with perspiration and his breathing down to a minimum, strained to hear what they were saying. Those freakin' crickets chirping, the ceiling fans, all the whispering, and what in the world broke? It nearly burst his eardrum through the listening apparatus! He swore under his breath. At least he could tell from this vantage point Jessica was still on the couch and not being whisked off to the hospital. So it didn't have anything to do with that.

He talked to Dr. White briefly during the fuss around Jessica earlier. "All of that business must have been a false alarm. What a drama queen! Hadn't women for the last 4000 years, in Asia, had babies right out in the middle of the sugar cane fields and gone right back to work?" He expected so much more from her; she always acted so tough around him.

Jude came in the house in a fluster to get the patio broom and dustpan. She had to walk past both boys to do so. She felt like a teenager the way they were looking at her. "Move," she said, as she sashayed between both of them, ponytail swinging. "I need to get that glass up," she said directly. Their heads turned to follow her, but their bodies didn't move. When she came back by, she looked at Jackson and said, "The trash can? Please."

"Uhhh, yes, ma'am. I'll get it … dear," he whispered out of the corner of his mouth, choking on laughter until she gave him the "mom" look (one eyebrow about four inches higher than the other one "look"). He grabbed the trash and followed her out, stopping long enough to pretend he was helping Spencer get his jaw off the ground.

Spencer threw his hands up dramatically, shaking his head mumbling, "What next?" He went back in to check on Straps. She was struggling to get up from the couch.

"Madam," he said dramatically, holding one forearm forward like a monkey bar. She evidently knew what to do with it. She put both hands on it, and he pulled her up like they had rehearsed it a thousand times. "You okay?" he asked her, as he took a sip of tea from his glass that was starting to make a watery ring on the ceramic coaster.

"Yep. Just need to stretch my legs and go and see a man about a dog." They both laughed as she waddled down the hall with both hands on the small of her back. He grabbed the remote control and started surfing all of his own favorite channels. He was very much at home here.

Daniel began to pick up the bigger pieces of the broken cup as he waited for Jude to return. He was quite pleased with himself. Sometimes you just have to wing it. Those boys didn't bother him one bit. Having them actually see it was better than two or three awkward talks and uncomfortable moments. It was out there now—way out there. He was happy that guys don't have the need to go to the park and spread out a quilt and talk for eight straight hours about their feelings like girls do. They took one look and BAM! They got the whole picture in a matter of seconds.

With the mess swept up and the broom returned to its closet, Jude ran upstairs to change out of the coffee-stained jeans. She unwound the strappy gold sandals and left them on the floor next to her blue velvet antique dressing chair in the bathroom. She went into the closet and kicked the jeans in the general direction of the hamper.

At times like this, she really missed having a housekeeper. She was in a hurry to get back to her guests. She smiled as she glanced in the mirror, twisting and pulling into a pair of black leggings. She looked at herself for a minute as she "hopped" them up the rest of the way. She quickly freshened up her perfume and was tempted to slide down the banister to expedite getting to the den, back to the family, back to where Daniel was. She gathered her wits and decided one step at a time might be the wisest decision.

She lit a few vanilla candles on the hearth as she made her way to the overstuffed chair. Jackson came in to join them, and Spencer tossed him the remote. Daniel came in from washing the coffee off of his hands, sat down in the recliner and kicked the footrest up. She smiled as she looked at everybody relaxed and comfortable. She leaned over into the blanket basket and grabbed a soft, pink afghan and tucked her feet up under her. Jackson punched up the volume, and they all cozied up to watch the news.

As their favorite newsman with the plastic hair began his report on Greece, they all paid close attention.

"Greece has fallen in the wake of previously exiting the Eurozone. Their Parliament has tried desperately to remain independent; however, they have exhausted all of their resources. As of 3:00 p.m. today, they announced complete bankruptcy and shortly thereafter, the European Union took total control in an effort to stabilize the projected ripple effect. The previously fallen economy is being hailed as the main contributor to their lack of fortitude, and unfortunately, this will have a huge impact on many countries' economic state. These events have put a huge spotlight on worldwide currency and have the ability to render devastation on the U.S. as well."

The report was interrupted by Spencer's phone buzzing and vibrating on the coffee table. Jackson muted the television. "Spencer," he said dryly. "Yeah. Okay. I'm not at home, so it'll take a little longer. I'll need to go pick up the van and a casket. I'll leave now. Okay. Yep. Yep. Headed out now." Daniel pushed the footrest as he pulled the handle on the side of the recliner and stood up.

"You got a pickup?"

"Yeah. Man, I wish we could do that test run with the C-casket."

"Why can't you?" asked Jackson.

"We don't have a Guinea pig. We need somebody to actually ride in the bottom of it."

Jude spoke up, "What do you think about me?" She put both hands on her chest.

"NO," everybody in the room shouted at once.

"Mother, that's crazy! I'm not letting you be a Guinea pig for anything like that. It's a test for Pete's sake. We don't even know if it will work!"

"Okay, okay, guys," Jude conceded, putting her hands up in surrender. "Don't everybody jump down my throat. I was just offering to help."

"And we appreciate it, Jude," Daniel defended, "but I'll have to agree with Jackson on this one. It's just not safe."

Jackson snapped his fingers loudly. "I have an even better idea." He pointed at Spencer. "I have a weighted jacket. It looks like the vest they put on in an x-ray room to limit exposure. I actually made one similar for weight training. It's about 150 pounds. Would that be about right? Will that work for the test run?"

"Oh, gosh, that's perfect," said Spencer, getting excited. "That's close enough to the weight requirement. You got it here?"

"Yeah, it's upstairs, I'll run get it."

"Okay, I need to get a move on," he shouted after him. "They time me!" Jackson was already halfway up the stairs.

Daniel looked at Jude and put his hand on her shoulder. "He doesn't have time to take me all the way to Aurora. Looks like I'm here for the night, if that's all right."

"Looks that way," Jude said grinning. "I'll put fresh towels in the guest room. Oh, it's got its own private bathroom. It's next door to Jackson's room. I'll show you in a bit."

"I hate to impose," he said softly.

"Shhhh." She shook her head looking up at him. "It's no problem, I promise. I'm happy for you to stay."

"Yeah," Jackson reassured him, as he came back down the stairs, "don't worry about it, man." He clapped him on the back. "Mom makes a mean stack of pancakes."

"It's no imposition for us, I promise," agreed Jessica. "The more, the merrier. Maybe there'll be another earthquake or something." They all looked at her, puzzled.

"What, Crazy?" Jackson said (he always called her that when she said something stupid).

"I'm just trying to keep things light and exciting," she remarked, as she headed towards the stairs to go to bed. "What with all the kissing and labor pains and what not, you just never know. Be careful, Spencer!" she yelled, as he opened the front door to leave.

"Always am," he said back, as Daniel tossed him his car keys.

Jude showed Daniel his accommodations for the night and put an extra folded quilt on the chair next to the bed. "It gets pretty chilly in here; we like it ice cold," she said smiling.

"So do we," Daniel replied, emptying his pockets onto the dresser. "It's perfect," he said. "I really appreciate it." He looked so tall standing there in front of the mirror.

"I'm happy you're here," Jude said, as she headed toward the door. The room felt like it was starting to get smaller by the minute as he began unbuttoning his shirt. She turned to tell him goodnight, but before she shut the door, he smiled at her and said, "Tomorrow, we'll talk about that kiss."

"Okay," she agreed, and winked at him as she quietly shut the door.

"Now, who's being the girl?" Daniel asked himself, as he looked at the flowered quilt in the chair.

Chapter 24

An Opportunity

Spencer pulled up under the porte-cochère at the funeral home where they load and unload the bodies. He rolled the casket out on the "church trucks." He had no problem getting it into the back of the van. Even with the added 150 lb. weighted vest tucked away in the hidden compartment, he got it pushed in easily.

He had waited patiently for the right opportunity to execute this plan. Everything had to fall into place; he couldn't make any mistakes. Timing was of the essence *and* his upper body strength. He locked the back of the van and placed both hands on either side of the double doors. He looked up at the heavens and said aloud, "You know I'm gonna need special protection tonight, right, Lord?" He went around and climbed in the driver's seat and drove out of the parking lot clutching a travel mug full of hot coffee. The moonlight shown overhead, lighting the way. He never saw Tony's surveillance van pull out behind him, headlights turned off.

"Y'all get up," whispered a burly guard as he kicked a thick bedroll with his foot. Bob and Liz sat straight up. Bob feeling around for his glasses, silently motioned for Liz to follow. She jumped up and rubbed the soft stubble on her head. Her hair was just beginning to grow back in little blonde tufts. Her blue eyes strained in the darkness to see one foot in front of the other. *What now,* they questioned with their eyes, not speaking. No Camp rules had been broken, so why had they been dragged out of bed at this hour.

"Got one," grunted the guard as they followed him into Bunker House B. There was a body that needed to be taken to meet the funeral home van. They usually did it first thing in the morning, but for some reason, they wanted it removed tonight.

"I'll get the heavy end," Bob whispered, as he hoisted up the man underneath his shoulders. Bob was tall and stout and only in his 50's, while Liz was short and spry. She got a good hold of his ankles on either side of her waist, and they started the cumbersome trip of getting him the 120 feet through the long rows of military-type barracks. They got about a quarter of the way there, and Liz stopped and whispered into the darkness, "Let me get under his knees; it feels like he's slipping." Bob stopped long enough for her to readjust her burden, and they trudged on, carrying the dead weight of a no name person. In the C-Camps, they were assigned letters to signify their barracks A–F. Nobody had names anymore.

Spencer arrived at the Camp, hung his head out the window and flashed his ID at the gate guard. The gravel crunched under his tires as he slowly made his way around to the small cement block building. A thin cloud of dust rose from the dirt driveway, floating in the low beams of the van. His heart raced knowing just below the springs of the casket interior lay the weighted vest. Everything was riding on this trip. It could determine life or death for many of the unknown letters—hundreds of them, just a few feet away, asleep in the barracks.

He slung the gear shift in reverse and backed the van up as far as it would go until it butted the curb. He got out and let the door click shut. Then he walked to the back and punched the unlock button on his key chain, opened both doors and got the church trucks out. They were folded up and sprang like an accordion when he released the silver slide. Spencer positioned and locked the wheels and pulled the casket right out on top of it with no problem. He couldn't even feel the weight difference. He didn't know if it was sheer adrenaline or the trucks just absorbing the extra pounds, but he was relieved.

It was eerily quiet in the Camp, just the buzz of the electric fence and the sound of the squeaky wheels rolling as he guided the casket up the cement sidewalk. Nobody was out and about. Even the guards were too lazy to help tonight. There was a dim light just ahead under the door. He heard another vehicle pulling down the gravel drive but didn't stop to look. He was there to do a job and get out.

Spencer heard a heavy door creak open in a building adjacent to the one he was headed to. He let his eyes briefly glance over. He didn't want anybody sneaking up on him in his heightened state of "kick-butt" that he always got in this place. He didn't trust his reflexes. He would throw down just about anybody if they came at him. Beat up first, ask questions later. He wasn't getting stuck in this body dump. They'd have to take him out feet first!

A Suit came out and lit a cigarette. Spencer heard the strike of a match and could faintly smell the sulfur. He heard the other vehicle cut the motor and a door slam in the distance. He was freaking himself out, so he tried to refocus on the remaining three steps to the door. *"Oh, great! There's a spider next to the handle. I'd rather face a firing squad than a spider! Good, gosh almighty,"* he thought, *"can I just get the body and go already?"* As if the spider could read his mind, it leapt from the door to the ground, scurrying away.

Tony braced his back against the wall with one bent knee and watched the casket roll down the sidewalk. He finally put the pieces together of the shirtless wonder and his connection to the Camps. *"Okay,"* he thought, *"I get it now. They work with the 'stiffs' here, too."* Lucy, his dear old aunt at the funeral home, had made it as clear as mud of the connection. He lit his own cigarette off the red hot stump of the Suit's ashes, and they watched Spencer until he disappeared behind the door.

Spencer closed the door behind him, expecting to be alone as he always was. He hoped the spider stayed on the other side of the door. Movement right behind him made him jerk around! He squinted in the dim lights. "Bob? Bob Winters? Is that you? Oh, man, Liz?"

"Spencer?" they said, moving in to get a closer look. It was hard to recognize them with her lack of hair and his loss of weight.

"I didn't know you guys were even here! What happened? What'd they charge you with?" Spencer grilled.

Bob kept his voice in a hushed tone. "We tried to have church in our home. It didn't fly too well. We had a mole. The Suits came in one morning, said it wasn't technically against the law to meet in our home, but" he raised both arms and said, "they still brought us here."

Liz crept over to the window to peer out of the blinds.

"Liz!" Bob whispered, "come away from that window."

"I'm just seeing if we have any company," she replied.

Spencer shook his head in disbelief. "Since the church disbanded, Dad and I haven't seen anybody until now."

"Keep your voice down," Bob cautioned. "If they hear you, it could be bad for all of us. I don't want to see you land in this hole."

Spencer reached out to touch Liz's shoulder, but she pulled back. "We don't have any gloves or a lot of water to wash. I don't know what this guy died of, but let's play it safe."

"That's bull," said Spencer. "Here, I have extra gloves in the casket." He opened it up, and she took a pair. Her fingers grazed over his, and they both made brief eye contact. He saw for a fleeting moment a depth of sorrow in her eyes—but courage, too. "I hate leaving y'all here," he said.

Liz cleared her throat and responded. "Now, Spencer? Look at me, come on." It was hard on him to look her in the eyes, but he did. "I mean it. You can't do anything about this. We're okay, right, Bob?"

Bob nodded slowly in agreement and added, "We know the Lord sees us right where we are. Doesn't it say in the Bible that *all things work together for good?*"

"Yes, sir, but …."

"No but's. We trust Him. He always has a plan."

At that moment, a light bulb flicked on in Spencer's head. His face lit up. "I know what this is now," he pointed a finger. "We DO have a plan. With your help, we just might be able to pull this thing off."

"What can we do to help? We're stuck in here," Bob said, raising both hands in frustration.

"Well, that's the beauty of it," replied Spencer, starting to get a little excited. Bob and Liz moved in a little closer, and Spencer showed them the secret compartment. They both said they were anxious to help.

"Now Sherri, she'd fit. She'd be an easy load," said Liz. "She barely weighs 100 pounds now. What do you think, Bob?"

"Yeah," he agreed, "she'd be a good one, or there's that other Sherry." He crossed his arms and put his finger to his temple. "She and her son would be about the right size. They're in our barracks, too." He walked around the casket looking at it from all angles.

"I was thinking about you, Liz," said Spencer. They both froze. "I could take you right now," he said, sincerely.

"Not a chance," she said. "I can't leave him; I won't! 'For better or worse,' right, Bob?"

"Forget it, Spencer, she won't go," replied Bob. Liz started pacing around the small room.

"We'll have a plan for the next time you come. We'll get it organized," she whispered, clasping her hands and not really talking to them, but to herself.

"We should have a code so we can move at a moment's notice. We'll try to get their rolls moved over closer to the door," Bob suggested.

"Won't they notice they're gone?" asked Spencer.

"No," replied Bob, "they have really lousy records. They just assign the barrack letters; they don't go by names. They only glance in every now and then to check on crowding."

They continued to talk in hushed tones while they worked together to wrap the poor dead guy and place him in the casket, Liz wearing the new gloves. Bob was just about to speak when the door burst open.

"What in the Sam Hill's taking so long in here?" shouted the guard, as he roughly shoved the door open with his heavy boot. He and the

Suit stood right outside the threshold. They didn't want to get too close to the dead guy.

"Body fluid problems, sir," Spencer replied quickly. "Had to rewrap it." The guards took one giant step backwards away from the door. Bob and Liz stood still, side by side, eyes averted to the floor. They held each other's bare hand, the new gloves tucked quickly out of sight.

"Are you finished with them two?" asked the burly guard, motioning with his head.

"Yep," Spencer said, busying himself with the body wrap, careful not to glance over at them.

"Well, get out of here then!" the Suit spat out at them, and they both backed to the door, never looking up and disappeared into the night.

Spencer rolled the casket past all three of them. They all backed up giving him a wide berth, burying their noses in the crook of their arms just in case "B" had already begun to reek. Spencer wasted no time getting the van loaded and putting some distance between him and the big electric gate. Two turns, some rubber left behind at a couple of corners, and he was hauling it down Hwy 26. The Lord had done more than protect him tonight; He had orchestrated a divine appointment with his old Sunday school teachers from church! What were the odds? He slapped the dash of the van and glanced back at "B" and the weighted vest riding in the closed casket and nodded his head. He had a smile on his face and a new determination in his eyes.

Chapter 25

The Storm

Morning peered dark and gloomy through the window, stirring Jude from her dreams. It may have been a rumble she felt deep within the earth or was it something else? It only lasted a moment. Then the lightning cracked while the storm clouds gathered right outside of her window.

A flash of color caught her eye. The beautiful redbird once again was perched in the lofty heights of the oak tree singing away. She watched him for a moment as he stretched his perfectly feathered wings, then flew away into the dark grey sky.

She sat up on the side of the bed and remembered Daniel—downstairs, in her guest room. She picked up her reading glasses and looked at the time. 6:45 a.m. Perfect.

She slipped on her robe and slippers and went into the bathroom to brush her teeth. She pulled a comb through her hair and wadded it up in a shiny black clip. She dabbed on pale pink lip color from a tiny pot and slapped on a quick coat of mascara. As she started down the stairs, she could hear muffled voices below. Daniel, Jackson and Spencer were all at the bar drinking coffee, discussing Spencer's midnight run. Jude caught the tail end of the conversation as she went unnoticed to the counter. When she opened the cabinet to get a cup, they all looked up. Daniel immediately walked over to her. He gave her a quick hug with the boys watching them.

"Morning, Mrs. Cleaver," said Jackson, making the sign of circles around his face. He had noticed the morning lipstick. She could have killed him but instead crossed her brows at him. He didn't push it, just lighthearted teasing.

"Did you sleep well in the guest room?" she asked Daniel, playfully tuning Jackson out.

"Like a baby," he said. "That's such a comfortable bed, and those quilts were perfect."

"I'm so glad," she said, as she put her coffee pod in the machine. "Sure you didn't get too cold?"

"Are you kidding?" he said, relaxed, leaning against the counter in the same clothes he had worn last night. "That's exactly how we keep it at our house."

"Hey, Mom. You'll never believe who Spencer saw at the Camp last night," said Jackson.

"Who?" she asked anxiously.

"Bob and Liz Winters."

"Our neighbors, Bob and Liz?" Jude said, placing both hands on her chest.

"Looks like it," Spencer replied, while Jackson nodded him on.

"What a small world," said Daniel. "When the boys told me that this morning, and about their arrest, I felt so bad for them. I'm sorry you had to see all of that, too," he said, addressing Jude, compassionately touching her shoulder. "I had no idea they lived over here. We know them from church."

"Well, they've been our neighbors for years," Jude said, as she got a teaspoon out of the drawer. "Liz and I have served on fundraisers, the HOA committee and we organized the Yard of the Season Award Ceremony. I was so scared for them. I'm glad to hear they are at least okay."

They filled Jude in on all of the details of the plan and how Bob and Liz were eager to help. Jude's heart started pounding at the thought of the danger they would all be in each time they did a run.

"I wish I could help," said Jackson, shaking his head.

"I know you would love to help," said Jude, reaching over to touch his arm, "but if they saw you, you'd end up in the Camp yourself, and God only knows what they might do to you. A huge strike of lightning followed by a loud clap of thunder shook the house to its foundation.

They all grew serious as the lights flickered off and on, then another big crack of lightning zigzagged through the sky, flashing in all the windows. It started a downpour so loud, they all rushed to the front door to look out. The rain was coming down in massive sheets; they could barely make out the houses across the street. Another flash of lightning and then the hail started. It beat down on the roof and the funeral home van. Spencer had come straight over after the body drop and drove the van there. It was being pulverized.

Jessica came out of her room yelling, "Anybody here? Guys, it sounds like the wrath of Montezuma up here!"

Spencer walked towards the stairs where she was making her way down in her jeans and black tank top. "It's hailing like crazy! I'm glad all of our cars are in the garage."

"Thanks for making me park in the most likely place to get the most damage," Spencer joked. They all laughed a little, but then all went to the back door and walked out onto the covered patio.

Jessica was slow and took her time following. The hail and rain sounded twice as loud with the low ceilings. They could see the hail piling up in the yard. They had to shout to hear each other. It was crazy; the hail was as big as golf balls. Jude shuddered at the sound of the pounding on the patio roof and went in the house with Jessica. Daniel followed after her and called the funeral home and gave instructions regarding "B," as well as letting them know he wouldn't be in this morning. The phone lost its signal, so he just hung up and slipped it back into his pocket.

Jude made Jessica's coffee while Spencer and Jackson went into the den and clicked on the TV, hoping it still had a signal. They joined the boys as the weatherman was blaring out news of the hail storm and showing footage of the radar. The storm was nowhere near over. The radar showed rapid flooding and hail damage. The hail was expected to be short-lived with no end in sight for the rain. Everybody was instructed to stay where they were. Streets and businesses closed down as the waters rose.

They had never seen anything like this; it was crazy! The guys went back to the front door to see if the hail had slowed down. It sounded quieter on the roof. The streets outside were full of water and had begun to crest in the yards. The rain beat down with huge drops.

The water was halfway up on the van tires, but the hail had completely stopped. Jackson and Spencer grabbed umbrellas and went barefooted to assess the damage to the van. It was covered with dings. "At least it wasn't Dad's car. It would have already floated away!" shouted Spencer over the roar of the rain. Jackson nodded in agreement, and they both ran back to the house, the water sloshing over their ankles even on the walkway. They stood in the foyer and dripped while Jude got fresh towels. They were drenched.

"It's flooded, guys! We couldn't drive anywhere if we wanted to. We're locked in," announced Jackson.

The TV signal became weak with a lot of static, but they could easily keep up with what was being said. The newsman pushed his earset closer to his ear, and while the film still rolled, shouted, "What? Did I hear that correctly? Would you repeat that, sir?" The camera went to close-up on his confused face. The newsman looked like he'd seen a ghost. I'm sorry to have to report this terrible update, but ...." ZZZZZZZZZ ... The sound of loud static was deafening! zzzzzzzzzz. The TV crackled and popped ... zzzzzzzz ... Then it went to white noise only.

"What the ..." Jackson exclaimed, as he frantically flipped from channel to channel. Then it went totally black. Dead silence. Then the cable box flickered back on within a few seconds, and a blue screen replaced the black one. ERROR 777 flashed at the bottom of the screen followed by the message: THE SATELLITE SIGNAL HAS BEEN INTERRUPTED. IF IT CONTINUES, PLEASE CALL THE NUMBER OF YOUR SERVICE PROVIDER FOR FURTHER TROUBLESHOOTING.

More silence, and then a toolbar loading at the bottom of the screen gave them all renewed hope. It got to 80% and froze up. At this point, every man in the room was ready to put their fist through the screen. And then, like magic, it popped back on.

They all sat up on the edge of their seats to hear the broadcast. Every station blared the same thing: "I repeat," cried the newsman, "it has been confirmed that the President of the United States has been assassinated. A sniper's rifle hit its mark as the President was going from the White House to the helicopter, surrounded by the Secret Service and different department heads. He was the only one who was fatally shot. Reports have it that he was dead before he ever hit the ground."

They were all frozen in place. They couldn't even look up at each other; they just stared in disbelief as every channel broadcasted the terrible sequence of events. They watched like deaf mutes while the Vice President, refusing to place his hand on the Holy Bible, was sworn into office right there on the lawn, 20 feet from the pool of blood that was still staining the helipad crimson red. The TV went totally black. Jackson grabbed Jude's hand.

"Here we go, Mother. This is it." They all stood to their feet in shock. Daniel took Jude's other hand. She still clung to Jackson, and Jackson held Jessica's hand while Spencer stepped closer to Jessica. For one brief moment, they just stood in silence, letting it soak in, and the screen went blue.

"Spencer," Jessica said, "you're dripping water on my feet."

"It's not me, Straps," declared Spencer, stepping back, looking down at his clothes. I'm dry." They all turned and looked at her standing in a pool of water.

"Well, I guess it's me then, guys. I think my water just broke."

Chapter 26

A Time to Push and Hail to the King

"You gotta be kidding!" Spencer shouted, trying not to look at the fluid on his bare foot. "Is water breaking a bad thing or a good thing?"

"Mother!" was the only word Jessica could form.

"It's gonna be fine," Jude said, rushing to her and cupping her face. "Look at me, Jessica. We're not going to panic, do you hear me?" Jessica nodded, as she clasped both of her mother's wrists tightly. "Wait a minute," Jude said, putting her hand under Jessica's chin. "Hold it together. We can do this."

"But we can't leave the house, Mother!" shouted Jessica in a panic. "How are we going to get me to the hospital?" she demanded to know.

"Do you trust me?" Jude said.

"Yes, I think so," she replied, totally freaked out.

"Listen to me. Daniel can handle this. He knows what to do. We can't leave the house, baby. You have to do it here. He delivered many, many babies when he was in the Army. I'm here, Jackson's here, Daniel's our best shot," Jude reassured her.

"What about my epidural?" Jessica continued to panic.

"We got this, Sis. I'll stay right here with you if you want me here."

She clutched her brother's arm. "You have to stay! I don't think I can do this here!"

"We're doing this," he said strongly. "I won't leave you."

Spencer, wanting to do something besides fight the urge to faint, spouted out some nonsense about people having babies every day.

Jessica was quick on the draw and responded with, "Well, let's talk about that after you push a bowling ball out of, oh, let's say, one of your nostrils!"

At that moment, she nearly buckled under the crushing pain in her back. She moaned loudly, and Jackson scooped her up and said one word to his mother. "Where?"

Daniel, right behind them, followed Jude up the stairs to Jessica's room. In one big swoop, Jude threw the comforter off and turned the sheets back. "Wait!" Jude said, cocking her head to one side, looking suspiciously at Jessica. "When did you change these sheets last?"

"Mother, come on! Last night!" Jessica bellowed as Jackson laid her on the bed.

Jude sent Spencer to the garage for a roll of plastic, and he shouted as he bounded down the stairs, "I guess Jackson wasn't kidding about the garbage bags and rope!"

Tony and the rest of the Suits who had gathered for the big convention, cheered loudly as the news of the President went viral. They all held up their snake charms and forehead signs and started swaying and singing a song that sounded more like the "Mother Russia" song than anything sung in America.

At long last the day is here!
We sing to you, our King, so clear!
With serpent old and heart of stone
We crown you King and King alone!

There were over 800,000 Suits who had flown into Area 51 this morning from all over the world. A huge bonfire as tall as a two-story building burned brightly in the midst of the masses. Some were moved with emotion as they all joined hands in one accord, tears glistening in their eyes.

A robust determination grew in their hearts as three black limousines made their way through the throng of Suits towards the stage set just in front of the blazing fire. They all strained to see as a 20-foot length of purple carpet was rolled out to receive him. The driver of the middle car got out and opened the door. An ominous figure dressed in a black suit and a white turban stepped out and then another and another. They bowed low, reached in and took the hand of the King. He was tall and dark and also wore a black suit with a black velvet cape-like overcoat, but he wore no turban. He had on his head, a thin golden crown with a ruby-incrusted serpent curled around his forehead, disappearing into the thick dark locks of his hair that hung nearly to his waist.

The Suits roared as he was escorted to the center of the stage. The sound was thunderous until he raised his hand for silence forcing the cape off of one shoulder. The silence only lasted a moment as the Suits in unison began to lift their deep voices in song. They grew louder and louder as the renewal of their patriotic homage to the Serpent King exploded. Finally, after years and years of training and preparation, not to mention the personal sacrifices they all had made, the plan was coming to nirvana right before their eyes.

Tony's eyes filled with tears as he joined in the chorus. All the Suits began to move in closer and lay things at their King's feet. Whatever they had—pocket watches, coins, paper money. Some even took their rings off and handed them forward. The mound of offerings began to grow, and Tony smiled at the gift he planned on giving—the little gift that was due any day now—his firstborn son. A gold watch or all the money from the 401K's were great gifts, but a child, especially a boy, dedicated to the King, well, that would be the gift of all gifts.

"Breathe Jessica!" Jude encouraged, as they went through another grueling contraction.

"It's all in her back," Daniel whispered, as he rolled his latex gloves off. "It's the worst kind of labor you can experience." Jessica was drenched in sweat as the assault continued, crushing her lower back. Every contraction made it feel as if it were being broken in half. She would get a reprieve—then it would start again!

"Hee, hee, hi, hi," she blew. "Hee, hee, hi, hi!"

Daniel instructed: "Like you're blowing a candle out with each sound. Push with your belly. You're doing great, Jessica!" Daniel praised.

Another one started as she tried to do the "hee, hee" on her own but couldn't focus. "Somebody, help me!" she shouted. "Do y'all even know what you're doing?" she panicked, clawing at the sheets.

They all chimed in at once—even Spencer from 15 feet away at the door. "HEE, HEE, HI, HI!" they all chanted and puffed together as she struggled to get through contraction after contraction.

Jude dipped a washcloth in a basin filled with cool water and bathed her brow and neck.

"I need to get up!" Jessica demanded.

"UP?" Jackson questioned. "Come on Jess. Why?"

"I don't know why," she said, as she began to rise, not waiting for assistance. They all stood beside her as she slung her arms around Jackson's neck and hung, letting his shoulders and neck bear her weight while she stretched her back out. His face was serious as another contraction slammed her nearly to the floor.

"Please, Jess," he pleaded with her, as he effortlessly supported her underneath her arms looking from Jude to Daniel. "Please, let me lay you back down, Angel."

"Jackson! Just hold me up! HEE, HEE, HI, HI, HEE, HEE, HI, HI!" she shouted, struggling through one more agonizing contraction. "Okay," she panted, "lay me down."

Jude put a length of the plastic on the bed first and put two thick towels down over it. Then they helped her to lie back.

Daniel ran the boys out while he checked her again. "We're at a 7," he shouted! The boys cheered from the hall!

"How far do we have to count?" Spencer asked Jackson, breathless from the counting and heaving and "hee heeing." Both of their lips were already chapped.

"Just to 10," Jackson said, slapping him on the back. "We're a heck of a lot closer than we were 10 hours ago." They were worn out. They both nodded at each other and approached with caution as Jude settled Jessica back on the labor bed and sat on it herself, wiping Jessica's cheeks with the cool washcloth.

"Jackson, get your butt over here, now!" Jessica burst out.

"I'm right here, Sis."

"No, I mean grab my hand!"

Jackson just climbed right up in the bed beside her and let her squeeze his hand nearly off as nature propelled her in the delivery position.

"HE'S COMING!" she bellowed with deafening volume, as she grabbed Jude's hand as well and started bearing down. Daniel threw back the sheet, shocked that she had gone from a 7 to a 10 in less than thirty seconds with the baby crowning!

"Spencer!" Daniel shouted, "grab me those gloves and the scissors!"

"There is no freakin' way I'm coming over there!" argued Spencer, backing up.

"Spencer!" shouted Jessica, "you're in this, too!"

Spencer, as pale as a sheet, fumbled with the cardboard box full of thin medical gloves and felt for the scissors while avoiding the "business end" of all the activity. Daniel quickly pulled them on. At that exact moment, Jessica started pushing and straining and nearly panicked!

"Don't hold it back, Jessica!" shouted Jackson. "Scream all you want!" Jude could barely see through her tears as Jessica pushed and screamed the most blood curdling cry she had ever witnessed. Her knees went completely weak at the sound of her daughter in the age-old ring of fire as the baby's head came out while the thunder rolled and the lightning crashed all around the house.

"Oh, my God!" shouted Spencer, still holding the box of gloves, as the baby started crying, only the head out of his cocoon. Spencer wobbled backwards from the bed, dropping the gloves on the floor.

"Hold it together, Spencer," shouted Jude. "Come up here with me!" Spencer got to the head of the bed and braced himself against the wall.

"Now, the next urge you feel, Jessica," Daniel instructed, "push with everything you've got and hold it! Let's get this little boy out of there!" Her last scream tore through the rafters of the house penetrating to the very depths of the foundation as Jude and Jackson, helpless to do anything, held on tight and pushed her forward.

Daniel took the baby and wiped its little face and thick head of coal black hair. Jude and Jackson openly wept while Spencer stood in awe at what he had just witnessed, and *what in the world was he doing crying?*

"Is he okay?" Jessica asked, laughing and crying at the same time.

"Perfect," said Daniel, in quiet jubilation as he worked to cut the cord on the little wriggling baby he had laid on her tummy, "but evidently there's been a mistake."

He held the newborn up by the back of its neck and bottom, letting the blanket drop and said, "It's not a 'he,' it's a 'she.'"

Chapter 27

Pink

You could have knocked them over with a feather. *"A girl? How could this have happened in 2015?"* they all wondered. Jessica didn't care about any of that as she just stared speechless. "It's an actual baby," she said aloud. Everybody giggled.

"Yes, it certainly is," said Daniel, inspecting every nook and crevice, and getting her little feet inked up.

"No, seriously … that just came out of me … an actual baby!"

"Yes, Crazy, we all saw it," said Jackson, shaking his head.

"Who'd of thunk it?" said Jessica.

"Well, we all got a big surprise," said Jude. "Home delivery of a boy who turned out to be a girl. But you're right, you had an actual baby."

"Mother, all we have is boy stuff and no way to leave the house," Jessica commented.

"I don't think she'll know the difference, and we have tons of white baby T's and onesies for now," said Jude.

"We actually have to dress her?" Jackson asked. "She looks so darn cute just like she is."

"Now who's talking crazy?" Jessica teased.

Daniel wrapped her snug and put her in Jessica's arms. Jessica just stared at the little face looking up at her. She wasn't expecting this feeling at all. She didn't actually believe in love at first sight anymore, but there she was—hook, line and sinker. Two teardrops fell on the baby's face.

"What a surprise you are," she cooed softly, "and you're nowhere near 40 lbs." They all lightly chuckled, looking around at each other in the surreal atmosphere that comes with the birth of a baby.

"Well, Mother, Uncle Jackson, say hello to the newest member of our family: Grayse LaBelle Mitlow. We'll call her Belle for short."

Jude choked out a sob. Jessica nodded and held the tiny bundle up to her mother. Jude was overcome with emotion and cried softly as her thoughts drifted to Grayson. "Hello, little girl," Jude said softly, through her tears. "I love you so much. Welcome to our family." She stood for what seemed like forever, memorizing every detail of the tiny face, kissing and smelling her. The baby made little mewing sounds, and Jude's heart melted. She walked over to where Jackson was standing, and they both admired her together while Daniel washed up.

Daniel came out of the bathroom unrolling his sleeves and got the scissors and box of gloves and started for the door. "See what happens?" he said, playfully. "You deliver a baby and then it's 'let's just all forget about old Dan.' It's all about the baby." They all chuckled as he turned and motioned a perfectly still Spencer to come on. "Let's give them some privacy," he said, but Jessica spoke up.

"Guys, wait, how can I begin to thank you for what you have done for me today? Please, don't go. Y'all stay in here with us. Spencer, come look at her."

"Not before I hold her, Sis," said Jackson, taking her right out of Jude's arms.

"Beauty and the Beast," said Jude, knowing at that very moment he was smitten—ruined, in love with sweet baby Grayse LaBelle who all but disappeared in the crook of his arm.

Daniel, who was trying to be respectful said, "Are you sure? We don't mind stepping out."

Jude walked over to him and threw her arms around his neck. "How can I ever thank you?" she said.

He leaned back, put his hands on her waist holding her at arm's length. "Jude, this has been the best date ever!" They both laughed as she named all of the events out loud!

"Well, we had the broken cup 'incident,' you spent the night—inappropriate." He laughed out loud! "And then there's Jessica's water breaking on Spencer's foot. OH, and then you birthed my first grandbaby! It's going to be hard to top that, sir!" They all laughed heartily.

"Spencer?" Jessica strained to look around. "Where are you?"

"I'm right here behind you, still holding up this wall," he answered.

"Get over here where I can see you."

"Hey, I think we've all seen enough for one day," laughed Spencer.

She strained to look around to where he was still standing. "Come here, please," she motioned with her hand, still feeling emotional.

"Do we still have to mind her?" Spencer asked, looking over at Jackson handing the baby to Daniel.

"Well, maybe for the rest of the day, but that's it," he laughed.

Spencer sat on the edge of the bed and shook his head. "I guess this probably tops any of my plethora of funeral home stories I've collected over the years."

"You did good," she said softly.

"I don't know about that," he disagreed. "Your mom had to talk me off the ledge a couple of times back there."

"You still did what I asked, and you didn't faint and try to steal my moment, so we're all good? I wasn't too hard on you? You forgive me for the bowling ball quip?" she asked, as she grinned at him.

"After what I saw you do today, I'd say you were good on all fronts, Straps." She smiled at him and gently punched him in the arm.

"What was that for?" he asked.

She leaned over and whispered to him, "For seeing all my junk and nearly fainting! That doesn't help a girl's ego at all."

Spencer blushed and held up both hands. "I'm not touching that comment with a ten foot pole." They both smiled.

The men gathered around Jessica and admired the baby while Jude bustled around straightening the room and pulling the blinds to keep the flashes of lightning out of the room. It was still pouring down rain although they had barely noticed.

Daniel tried to hand the baby to Spencer, but he held up both of his hands in surrender. Not today, Dad, maybe tomorrow. I'm still rattled. Besides, I've got wallets that weigh more than she does. I will, however, hold her little hand." They all smiled tenderly as the baby latched onto his finger.

Jessica looked exhausted. Jude gathered up the refuse that needed laundering and started for the door. "Come on y'all; these two need to rest. Let's go downstairs, and I'll make those pancakes we never got around to. Oh, and Jackson, go to the game room and bring me the diapers and wipes." They all filed out, each taking a look back at Jess and the baby.

The sound of the city alarms started blaring loudly through the rain. "I'll bet it's a tornado warning," said Daniel, trying to yell over the noise.

"Yeah, or flood warnings or something like that," agreed Spencer.

After Jackson delivered the baby items to Jessica's room, he went straight to the den to see what all had happened with the assassination and new President or anything else that might have transpired over the last several hours. Thankfully, the TV came right on, no blue screens, and it was news on every channel. The Vice President, now Mr. President was on the face of every channel. "We are deeply sorry for the tragedy that we as a country are faced with. Let me assure you we will not rest until all of those responsible have been brought to justice." As he left the podium surrounded by all men in black suits, Jackson and Daniel just glanced over at each other seeing the same thing at the same time—a close-up of the new President showed a flash of gold right beneath his blue tie. It looked like the serpent charms the Suits all wore.

A few minutes later, Jackson got an anonymous text. <BLOCKED CALLER ID> It had a video attachment. It was a little distorted, but he'd know that "cat" anywhere. It was a video of Tony at some public demonstration with a fire blazing in the distance. He knew it! Freakin' Tony! Tony was a Suit! He watched the short clip and wondered how long it would be before he had a run-in with him—how long before he came to Texas. "Well, come on, buddy," Jackson said, as he glanced up the stairs. "I dare ya."

Chapter 28

Circle the Wagons

On the way to the kitchen, Jude made a detour and ran up to her room to freshen up a bit. She washed her face, changed her clothes and took a moment to catch her breath. She felt like she had had the baby. It had been a long 24 hours, and it was beginning to take its toll on her and everyone else. On her way back to the kitchen, she quietly opened the door, peeking in on Jessica and the baby. They were both fast asleep. Jude smiled as she went into the kitchen and got out a big green mixing bowl and measured out the flour and cracked a couple of eggs for the pancakes. She heated her mother's old iron skillet until the butter sizzled. It made the best pancakes ever. She got out a couple of pounds of bacon and got everything going before making herself a cup of hot tea.

The guys, all in the den, began to speak in hushed voices about the Suits, the assassination and the President's golden necklace they had spotted. Daniel scooted up in his chair and put his forearms on his knees. "Guys? I feel like there's a big change coming. I really believe in my heart that the assassination and this Black Suit order are all related to a degree that none of us fully realize yet."

Spencer walked over and looked out the window into the pouring rain. He could barely make out a birdhouse close to the glass. "I have to agree. I don't know about you guys, but I think the next call I get to run out to the C-Camp, I'm gettin' somebody. I mean it! This is only about to get worse. I'm so ready to get even one person out of that place." His mind drifted to Bob and Liz, and he wondered how they were faring in the rainy conditions.

Jackson stood by the fireplace leaning one arm on the hearth. "I think one of you guys needs to hide me in the van, and we make a practice run out to Decatur to see if it's safe for little Belle and Jessica."

Daniel had gotten up and strolled over to where he was. "Seriously, Daniel," Jackson said, "how soon will Jessica be able to move without causing any physical problems?"

Daniel scratched the back of his neck for a brief second and said, "I think if we wait three days, make sure everything's functioning properly."

"What are you talking about, Dad?" Spencer interrupted.

"Huh, Spencer?" Daniel said, and glanced around to make sure Jude wasn't in earshot. "Milk, blood loss, bathroom functions," he whispered.

"Stop, stop! I get it." Spencer waved him off. "I've got the picture."

Jackson had his face screwed up, too.

"There are just some things you don't need to know, aren't there, Spencer?" Daniel said with a grin on his face.

They both shook their heads in agreement, and then Daniel stopped and put his fingers over his mouth and squinted his eyes, like he was deep in thought.

"Just how far did you say it was to your place in Decatur?" Daniel asked him.

"I'd say it's about 45 minutes," Jackson answered. "Why? What are you thinking?"

Daniel cradled one of his elbows and pointed his index finger at Jackson. "Well, you know, I mentioned our place in Aurora. We haven't had any activity out in our area there as far as the Suits go. You know, small town and all."

"Yeah?" Jackson said, just listening.

"Now, this is just a suggestion." He held one hand up, stop-sign fashion. "We don't want to get a moving truck or anything to draw attention, but what do you think about relocating your sister to my house until we check out your Decatur place and make it comfortable and well stocked?"

"Oh, wow," Jackson said slowly, pulling his head back and putting his hand over his heart. "I can't imagine not being the one watching over them," (Daniel nodded while Jackson digested the information) "but that actually makes a lot of sense. I still need some time to wrap my mind around it first, but that's the best idea I've heard." He invited both of them to sit down. He had something serious to tell them and show them.

They sat down, and Jackson tossed Spencer his cell phone. "First, let me tell you a little story about Tony, Jessica's so-called husband." He told them everything. Spencer's nostrils flared as Jackson told of the pain Tony had caused her. Then he told of the sighting when he personally had glimpsed him at the coffee shop by the gym. "At the time, I questioned if it was him or not. He'd disappear after just a glimpse; however, I started to put the pieces together when I received this disturbing video clip."

Daniel spoke up and said, "He does sound like a terrible person, but is he really a danger or threat or just a deadbeat husband?"

"See for yourselves," Jackson said, and nodded at Spencer to press play on his phone. The convention footage began to roll with an up-close and personal of Tony himself worshiping the cloaked figure near the blaze.

"That's Tony?" asked Spencer.

Jackson nodded, "In the flesh."

"Shh ... listen ... this is indeed grave," said Daniel, turning up the volume. He started speaking in a language that took Jackson by surprise. "It's not safe here for her and especially with a new baby. This Tony character can't be trusted."

"Uhh," said Jackson, "you can understand what they're saying?"

"Yeah," replied Spencer, "we probably haven't mentioned it, but Dad speaks Arabic, Spanish and perfect Cantonese."

"Well, what were they saying?" Jackson asked, still trying to digest what he just learned about Daniel.

Daniel swallowed and slowly said, "He said they were heading to Texas right away."

"That sorry piece. He'd better not get anywhere near this place," Jackson spat out as he pounded his fist against his other hand.

They all three ventured to the window; the rain making it hard to see out.

"There's something dark and sinister going on here, guys," said Daniel. "I know it, and y'all know it, too. I think if he comes here," Daniel hesitated, "as in right here," he said, pointing both fingers down, "something awful could happen."

"That's the odd part," said Jackson, pressing his head against the glass, straining to see out the window, "I've got the strangest feeling he's already here."

Chapter 29

The Serpent Crown

A beautiful rainbow was now visible from the window seat Tony squirmed in. The rain had just about stopped over Dallas. The 747 had circled around the DFW area in a flight holding pattern for what seemed like hours. Tony had long ago grown impatient about the cell phone rules the flight attendants struggled to enforce.

He was fed up. He replayed the video clip he anonymously sent Jackson. He had watched it probably 15 times. He chuckled to himself about how Jackson must see him now, in this light. He wondered if he'd climbed back under the bed yet. His shoulders shook with restrained laughter as he fantasized at how he would walk into the dark, damp interrogation room, Jackson probably handcuffed to the wall. Maybe he'd have them blindfold him, witch slap him a few times with one of those blackjacks—maybe until a few of his teeth lay on the ground. See who the tough guy was then.

He hit play one more time and nearly reached his higher ground letting the whole scenario play out in his mind. Maybe he would wait until Jessica popped that kid out, and before delivering him as promised to the Serpent King, let it squall about two feet away from Jackson. That would be the day of reckoning—HIM holding all the proverbial cards, and Jackson crumpled in a heap of chains, powerless to do anything.

The pilot crackled across the intercom instructing everybody to fasten their seat belts as they were about to begin their final descent. Tony put his phone away and watched out the window as the big plane's wheels hit the runway with a loud screech, doing what felt like 500 miles an hour.

Jackson found Jude in the kitchen handwashing a skillet. "Hey, Mother. Daniel, Spencer and I are going to go see what Decatur looks like after all of this rain. I'm hoping it's not all flooded. We need to get it ready and start moving people into it. Use it for what Dad and I designed it for."

"You're not talking about your sister, are you?" she said, over her shoulder, "because I'm not sure if she could stay out there by herself, are you?"

"No, Mom, we may have another temporary solution for her and the baby, but we're gonna do whatever it takes to keep her safe. There's something else, Mother. Your first reaction probably won't be too great, just warning you, but try and keep a level head."

"Well, now you're scaring me," she said, as she turned around and grabbed a towel to dry off her hands. She took off her apron and crossed her arms, leaning against the counter behind her and took a breath. "Okay, now, I'm ready to hear it."

He loved that about her. She was no shrinking violet—not when push came to shove. She'd shove you right back. She just needed a chance to brace herself. He told her everything, from the first time he saw Tony to the video. He told her of Spencer seeing him at the Camp, the President who wore the snake charm of the Suits, Daniel's invitation to move Jessica and Belle to the house in Aurora—everything. She listened as the events unfolded, and it started becoming clear what they needed to do.

"I agree. We need to get them out of here. I think we all should go for a couple of weeks and let things settle down here in town. Maybe by then, we'll no longer be on anybody's radar, and we can see the reality of living in Decatur."

"Mom, I think that's the route we need to go. We won't do anything here, like pack or anything. Nothing to draw attention. All the bills are paid up, the yards all look about the same with the chaos going on around us. I don't think anybody will even notice we're gone."

"I'll ask Daniel and Spencer if they want to go with us as well or if they need to keep up appearances at the funeral home so we can continue on with the C-Camp rescues," Jude said.

"Yeah, I knew you'd be on board. It's happening, Mother. I'm talking about the beginning of the end. I think this is really it. It's all about to go down."

Jude shuddered as they talked. "I know," she said, "I'm anxious to see what the new President is going to implement. If he's really one of those Suit guys, we're all in trouble. When can we move the girls?"

"Daniel said three days," replied Jackson.

Jude took a deep breath and shrugged her shoulders. "I'm totally onboard for all of it. Just tell me when I can start preparing her. She's gonna flip when she hears about Tony."

"Yeah," Jackson said, "flip out her .38 revolver."

"Guys," shouted Daniel, "get in here. They just showed a helicopter about to land at the White House. All networks have tuned in; must be a big deal."

"In Washington," the familiar, plastic-haired newsman announced, "we are anxiously awaiting the arrival of an 'unknown guest.' All the stops have been pulled out for this dignitary, and it's assumed he is of great importance. Over 200 of the Black Suits have gathered to meet him at the helipad and have made a receiving line on either side of the walkway to honor him all the way to the threshold of the guest entrance."

The camera panned over the growing crowd as the helicopter landed. The President could now be spotted heading toward the pad, surrounded by Secret Service and Suits as the whirling helicopter blades propelled it to a perfect landing. They waited until the blades completely stopped turning and the President was within 20 feet of it before placing portable steps for an easy exit for the highly esteemed guest. They could have heard a pin drop as the doorman put his hand on the handle and flung back the helicopter door.

"Oh, my God," shouted Jackson, "it's those guys from the text video!" Two ominous figures dressed in the black suits and white turbans stepped out. Again, the purple carpet was rolled out for the service of the King. A hush fell over the crowd, including the newsrooms, as hands were held out to help him down the portable steps. He looked as glorious and ominous as he had on the video. His long, jet black hair blew up three feet as the breeze blew through it, and he stepped out of the helicopter onto the purple carpet. He was wearing the black cape overcoat and this time had on mirrored sunglasses. There was no denying the thin gold crown on his head bore the image of the same serpent all of the Suits wore, except his was jeweled. Even the newsman was at a loss for words.

The same chill that was racing up Jude's spine, raced through every television set in America. The darkness penetrated across the airwaves and nobody spoke. The President went forward and took one knee, bowing before him, then waited until the King touched his head before he arose. *"Who is the American President bowing down to?"* was on every mind in the world. At that precise moment, ISIS broke through the Mexico/Texas border with such ominous numbers that the border patrols were overwhelmed. They marched, "tanked," "scud missled" and shot through the lines until every border patrolman lay dead.

Daniel fired up the van and backed it into the garage. Jackson stowed away where the transport casket was. He got the creeps a little but shook it off. No sense in creating any more drama. He had his AR-15; they weren't screwing around. If they were discovered by the Suits, they wanted to be ready. Daniel strapped on his Judge, and Spencer laid a shotgun in between the box seats of the van. They were jetting up Hwy 287, and it wasn't long before they were veering off the road towards the hideout.

Chapter 30

Be Still My Heart

"Yep. It's a muddy, slippery mess," Jackson thought, as they sloshed and bounced through the mud.

"Looks like it's only flooded in the low spots," commented Daniel.

"Good," said Jackson, as he pulled up to squat between the two box seats. "Pull in here."

They made it to the off-road Jeep, and before long, the hideout was in sight. The ground here was slightly elevated and dry. "Dad thought of everything," Jackson thought, as he handed them both headlamps.

"Wow," Spencer said, after the tour. "This is cool as heck! How did you come up with all of this?"

"Well, it was mostly my dad," answered Jackson.

"He certainly had a vision," Daniel replied. "I say, let's honor him and put it to good use."

Jackson stuck his hand out, and Daniel took it. "Thank you for saying that. My dad had no idea what we were all about to step into, but he had a dream. We worked on it for years. He'd be glad to know we were using it for the greater good. Well? Have you seen enough?"

Daniel nodded, and before long, they were back in the van rushing back to Colleyville. Spencer's phone rang.

"This is Spencer," he answered. "Yeah, yeah. Cool if I make a detour? My old man's with me," he said, trying to sound cool. His heart was pounding with the implication of maybe getting to do a rescue! "Oh?" He sat up straighter and looked at Daniel, panicked. He looked back at where Jackson was hunkered down and started shaking his head no! "Are you sure?" he asked the phone receiver. "It wouldn't take but a minute to drop him off."

He tried to keep his voice at an even keel—not show the panic he felt rising up in his chest. *"Freaking Jackson in the back, and us rolling into*

Camp with machine guns and mud slung halfway up the van. That won't look suspicious?" he thought, sarcastically. "Okay, I understand," he said, nostrils flaring. "I'm headed your way."

He had to submit; he had no choice. "Crap!" he shouted, after he clicked "End Call." "It can't get any worse!" he ground out.

"Oh, yes, it can!" yelled Jackson. "If I get taken into custody or worse—my mom and the girls ....!"

"Wait a minute, guys. We have a few minutes. Let's not waste it on the 'what if's.' Let's get you hidden, big guy. Spencer, take the wheel."

Daniel slowed down enough to exchange places with Spencer in the driver's seat of the van with the vehicle going 45 mph. He grabbed a cardboard air tray casket that was unassembled and started ripping the plastic bands off of it. "It's what we ship bodies in when we have to air flight them state to state," said Daniel quickly, without looking up. Jude had told him in a passing conversation that Jackson was claustrophobic, but this was the only possible way to hide him. He worked as fast as he could. They neared the turnoff to the Camp.

Jackson looked at the width of the cardboard casket. "You're going to put me in that thing? It's going to be a tight fit," exclaimed Jackson, shaking his head as he looked into the narrow box.

"I can get you in there," Daniel said with confidence. "It's not my first rodeo. It'll be tight, and it'll be dark, but we can make this work. Just remember: slow steady breaths; keep your eyes closed."

"Dude, are you sure?" he asked warily, breaking into a cold sweat.

Daniel stopped for a brief moment, putting his hand on Jackson's shoulder, saying, "Yes, I'm sure. Now, get in."

Spencer flashed his ID at the guard gate, and the big electric fence began to open. "For gosh sakes, have you got him sealed up yet, Dad!?" The steering wheel in Spencer's hands felt like somebody had doused it in olive oil. Daniel didn't respond. He was working as fast as he could as the gate shut behind them.

Jackson was trying to keep it together. All of their lives depended on it! He lay back in the cardboard casket on a thin, white casket blanket and pillow that immediately started absorbing the sweat pouring off of his body.

The look in his eyes was unmistakable and gave Daniel pause. The gravel crunched under the tires as Spencer slowly made his way toward the pickup station trying to give them time.

"Have you sealed him, Dad? Or are you going to read him a bedtime story!?" he whispered loudly out of the corner of his mouth while trying not to look back. It was daytime, and there were guards everywhere and a few scattered Suits.

Before Daniel put the lid down over it, he touched Jackson's folded hands. "You can do this, soldier. You can do it for your mother. You can do it for your sister and little Belle. They're counting on you."

"Blindfold me then, and shut the lid," said Jackson.

"For Pete's sake, close it, Dad!" hissed Spencer.

Daniel rolled off some clear packing tape and secured the lid as the van pulled to a stop. Spencer was nearly in full-blown heart failure by the time Daniel jumped into the passenger seat as he was shifting into Park. His dark eyes met his dad's as he got out of the van. He was rattled. Two big burly guards strolled up to the back of the van where Spencer was opening the big double doors. The fleshier of the two stamped out his cigarette butt, twisting a boot over it and wiped the sweat off of his own brow with the back of his meaty hand. Spencer noticed they both wore serpent charms and one wore rosary beads as well. "Hey!" he said, looking around, his large head moving from side to side. "Stop, right there!"

"What?" Spencer said. "Stop what?" All Spencer wanted to do was get the church trucks and the casket out and shut the doors with his dad and Jackson safely inside.

"Who's that?" Fleshy said, as he peered up through the back of the van. Jackson's heart caught in his throat from inside the dark cardboard coffin.

Spencer, trying to keep his hand from shaking, easily responded with, "That's my dad."

"Your dad?" he said sarcastically, contorting his face and sneering at the other guard. "Well, we'll just see about that," said the other guard. He opened the passenger door and jerked Daniel out by his shirt and slammed him face-first up against the van.

"Hey!" yelled Spencer, lurching forward as he saw the blood on his dad's lip. Fleshy grabbed him, then spat on the ground.

"Hold up, Catholic," he said to the other guard. "You got somethin' to say, boy?" the guard asked, as he vice-gripped Spencer's upper arm.

Daniel was as cool as a cucumber. He was trained for capture, combat—whatever they had in mind. He looked at Spencer and slightly shook his head "no," as in "don't go off halfcocked. We're putting off nervous energy, and they're picking up on it. Keep cool … stay calm … nobody has to get hurt here today." He said all of that with just his eyes.

Spencer immediately took a deep breath and said, "No, sir. I was just going to tell you that Command gave me permission to bring him. We were making another run when I got the call, and he didn't want me dropping him off first."

"Well, I'm gonna check your story out, and we'll go from there," he said, releasing Spencer's arm and shoving him forward. "Why don't you run along and do what you're here to do, and we'll see how 'daddy' plays out."

He smiled and looked at his buddy, and Spencer released the slide on the church trucks instead of releasing the cry of the banshee which was what was rising in his throat. He took another deep breath to regulate his breathing and pulled the casket out with Fleshy still at the back of the van watching. He wanted so bad to shut the doors, but the guard obviously was having much more fun toying with him.

"What's in there?" he asked, pointing with his large head at the cardboard casket.

Spencer was at the end of his rope. "A rotting corpse. Would you like me to open it for ya?"

The guard changed his mind and said, "No way, smart mouth." He stepped back for Spencer to pass. "Just go on and get the body."

Spencer didn't even look back. He rolled the casket into the little cement block building. Bob and Liz crept out of the shadows. None of them spoke until the door was securely shut. Spencer leaned back against it trying to regain his composure.

"What's your dad doing here?" whispered Bob, concerned. "I saw it all through the blinds."

"It's a long story, but I just hope we all make it out of here alive today." Spencer realized what he had just said and started to apologize to Bob and Liz, but they both looked at him with an "It's okay, we're where we're supposed to be" look.

"Can you still take her?" asked Liz.

"Who?" Spencer asked, still leaning against the door. Then he saw her standing there—dirty, bald, scared. "Today?" Spencer said, a little rougher than he would have liked. With all the drama, he had forgotten about the real reason they were all in the van today. The room grew quiet. He looked the woman up and down. "Are you sure we're ready to do this?" he questioned.

Liz looked at him and shook her head, and said, "But it's up to you." They all worked together to wrap the dead man. Bob and Liz told Spencer which building the officers were usually holed-up in. Bob had privileges in the building serving them. They wanted to help bring the C-Camps down and could unlock a few doors at a moment's notice should the opportunity present itself.

Spencer wordlessly nodded toward something in the casket. He had secreted a small revolver by the pillow. Bob grabbed it and stuffed it down the back of his pants. If things continued to escalate around the world, he didn't know if there were enough guards to maintain the integrity of the camp. "We'll be ready," said Bob, as he patted the gun under his clothing.

Spencer wanted nothing more than to first, get back to the van; two, get the heck out of that gate and leave this hellhole behind him; and three, get his dad and Jackson to safety. It was all on him. He had to move.

He came out of the block building, relieved to see Daniel back in the passenger seat and the two guards leaning back on the side of the van. It felt like slow motion as he made his way down the sidewalk. He bent to hoist up his heavy load and a wheel caught on a jagged piece of concrete, nearly jarring the casket off the trucks! Another three inches, and it was going to fall! One of the guards instinctively stepped forward and grabbed the handle just before the whole thing crashed to the sidewalk. Spencer rammed his leg under it and braced it as well. The guard let out a whole string of curse words as he smashed his fingers between the casket and the door of the van. They heave-hoed until they got it pushed in.

"Man!" the guard spat out, nursing his injured hand, "that's a heavy one. He sure didn't look that heavy this morning."

Spencer didn't respond, nor did he take the time to lock the coffin down. He just slammed both doors shut and climbed into the driver's seat. He could have won an Oscar as he smiled and nodded at the guard opening the big, heavy gates.

Dead silence. Neither of them said a word until they were safe outside of the electric fence. The Camp was disappearing in the big, square side mirror. He was blazing a trail. "Are you okay, Dad? Jackson?" he shouted. "Hang on, man! I'm getting us out of here!"

Daniel rushed to the back of the van, peeling and ripping the thick strips of tape off as fast as he could. Jackson began groaning like he was lifting a thousand pounds as he strained against the lid.

"Get me out of here!" he shouted through the darkness. Finally together, they had the lid off, and Jackson sprang up, gasping for air and soaked to the skin. Daniel helped him out, and he fell back, gulping air. They all began to laugh a little—that non-funny, nervous laugh—as they looked at their various conditions. Spencer, near a nervous breakdown, Daniel's busted lip and torn shirt and then Jackson sweating as if he was in the Watergate trial. They put as much distance between them and the C-Camp in the shortest amount of time possible.

Fifteen hundred yards away, a big armored truck, still running, was parked at an angle. A Uniform aimed his RPG7 at the approaching van. Tony squatted down beside him and raised his sunglasses. "Wait for it … wait for it," he whispered, to the Uniform. "Don't actually hit the van, just get close. Let them get in range." The Uniform wiped the sweat from his brow and prepared to fire the Hand Grenade Launcher.

The road exploded right in front of the van, sending sheets of asphalt and tree roots 40 feet in the air. The van went airborne as it careened off the side of the road. It flipped twice and skidded several feet before finally coming to rest on its side. As the dust settled around them, Daniel was the first to move. He unbuckled himself, nearly falling on Spencer. Daniel examined himself but had only minor cuts and bruises. Spencer, however, was barely conscious, but still very much alive with blood dripping from a large gash on his forehead. Daniel turned around to see Jackson checking himself for wounds, but he appeared to be fine with nothing bleeding. He had been wedged between the van and the casket, and it had actually secured him during the roll. Daniel gave him the universal sign for "silence" as he located Spencer's shotgun and crept back up to the passenger window which was now facing the sky. With the key still engaged, he pressed the window button and rolled it down. Gingerly raising his head enough to peek out, he could vaguely see in the distance what appeared to be an armored vehicle fleeing the scene.

They waited until the coast was completely clear, then they squeezed around the casket that was now lying on its side and made their way to the back of the van. They both put their feet on one of the doors and pushed in unison until it gave. Daniel rolled out silently, military fashion, and Jackson followed in an Army crawl on his elbows to where he was crouched behind a clump of earth. They glanced back at the van where one of the tires was still spinning. They both slowly raised their heads to peer over the mound of dirt but couldn't see anybody—just a huge gaping hole in the street and trees blown up everywhere.

Spencer started moaning from inside the van, and Daniel gave the silent motion for Jackson to go check. Jackson crawled backwards back into the van. Daniel secured the perimeter and went to investigate the point of impact. Spencer had already unbuckled himself and was muttering something about the casket.

"It's cool, man; it's still closed," Jackson assured him.

"No," groaned Spencer, "the girl."

"What girl? You're not making any sense."

"The girl in the casket."

"No man, that's a dude you picked up, remember? You hit your head. I think you're confused. Do you remember anything? We think there was a small bomb or something."

"Not a bomb," said Daniel, crawling back into the van, "it was a hand grenade. That was no accident; it was deliberate."

"Are you serious?" said Jackson, shocked.

"As a heart attack," replied Daniel. "They would have had to use a launcher of some sort, like the old bazookas." Spencer was still mumbling on about a girl. "Speak up, son," said Daniel.

Spencer finally got the words out. "Dad! I've got a girl from the Camp in the bottom of the casket!"

They rushed back to the casket, and Daniel said, "You pull, I'll push." Jackson got a good hold of the end of the casket. "We need to only slide it partially out."

"Got it," said Jackson, as he pulled and heaved, while Daniel pushed with his shoulders until they had the casket half in and half out of the van. Daniel located the casket key after a few minutes of searching in the mayhem of the van and began to crank the handle until it released. He warned Jackson to step back a little as he was still crouching down at the back of the van in the dirt. He stood immediately to avoid the stench or the sight, if there was any, from the un-embalmed remains that had been jostled around in the wreckage. Daniel flung it open. It was still wrapped and showed little, if no, harm from the turbulence. They had wrapped him well.

Daniel and Jackson picked up the body and laid it gently down and then reached in to remove the secret panel. There she was—wide-eyed and a little banged up, but she was virtually unharmed. She told them her name was Sherri. She couldn't believe they had done this for her.

"We gotta get out of here, guys," said Jackson, looking at the dirty girl. He was moved with compassion. Spencer, still holding a compress on his head, started to make his way out. They all crawled out of the back and knelt beside it to lift it back on its side. It wasn't a normal, hollow box van. It was commercial weight and extremely heavy.

"Wait," said Daniel. He stood up and held his hands out. "Join hands, guys." They did as he asked, and he bowed his head and said, "God, You see us where we are. We know Your hand was on us today protecting and guiding our every move. We trust that You'll be the fourth Man today, God, as we try and lift this van, like in the days of Daniel, Lord. Like Shadrach, Meshach and Abednego who were cast into the fire, but when their executioners looked in, there was a fourth like the Son of God in the flames with them. Be that fourth Man today and help us to get this van off the ground, and we'll give You the praise for it all. In Jesus' name."

They all squatted down with their hands under the van and Jackson said, "Let's get this thing up, men."

Chapter 31

Freedom

They all cheered when the van rolled into the parking lot where it sputtered and backfired and then gave up the ghost. Daniel led Sherri to the showers. She was filthy from the Camp, but her brown eyes were filled with hope. She was grateful for the soap, a hot shower and clean clothes (Jude had realized that the ones they rescued from the Camp would need fresh clothes, and she had gathered as many types and sizes of clothes as she could find and given them to Daniel. She went to quite a few different secondhand stores so she wouldn't arouse suspicion.). When Sherri was ready, Daniel gave her some food and water and a flashlight and quickly led her to the safety of the tunnel. She had everything she needed for the next leg of the journey. They'd be back to take her to Decatur later that evening. She rubbed the stubble on her head as she made her way through the tunnel and into the sanctuary of the beautiful mausoleum.

One down; many more to go.

They all went to Jude's, and Daniel patched up Spencer's head wound with a couple of butterfly bandages while they told her of their harrowing escape from the C-Camp. She was horrified at the close call. She warmed up a big pot of chicken soup, which they wolfed down. Then they called it a night, and Daniel and Spencer headed to Aurora.

She was ready to move, too. Things had gotten so precarious, anything could happen at any time now. She couldn't remember when their lives had gotten so far out of kilter. She had such an uneasy feeling. She couldn't pinpoint it, but something in the air just felt dark. She was ready to make the move and get her family safe in the hideout.

The next morning, Spencer was called out again and again. He had no idea what was going on, but he had three calls that day and then two more in the night. Bob and Liz had somebody ready each time, and with the van broken down, he made all the runs with their hearse. The Suits were too busy with whatever was going on there the last couple of days to bother him. Spencer had noticed more officers than usual, along with troops who appeared to be gearing up for something. He had gotten the other Sherry out, along with her son and five more, over the course of the day and night. They had him running nonstop for two more days. He had also decided that using the hearse was the best way to get them from the mausoleum to Decatur—nobody followed or pulled over a hearse. But just for safety sake, he made the women ride in two empty caskets, and the men cleaned up and just rode hunkered down. Spencer told them if they ever got pulled over, they would say they were headed to a double funeral, and the men wanted to ride with the body of their loved ones. It was the perfect plan. It meant several trips in the hearse, but when it was said and done, they had thirteen people safe and sound at the hideout.

They had already moved Jessica and Belle to Aurora to await transport to Decatur once Jackson could be out there full-time to protect them. Back at Jude's house, Jackson had gathered everything he could think of that they might need, and Jude stuffed a few more changes of clothes, all kinds of soap and candles, blankets, pillows and every canned good in the cupboards in cardboard boxes.

"Man, this is so weird," Jackson said, as he loaded the last box in the car they had moved into the garage. They had put the garage door down before they began loading the car. They didn't want to take any chances on someone seeing what they were doing. "Feels like we're leaving for good, doesn't it?"

"Yeah," Jude said, "I still can't believe it's come to this, but I'm ready to get out there. We can come back in a few weeks and get the rest of the things we think we need or can't bear to part with. I'm ready to organize everything and get everybody comfortable out there. We need to put some systems in place, like fire drills, a chore wheel and things like that." Jackson agreed.

"Are we going to take Jessica and the baby with us on the first trip out there?" asked Jude.

"Well, I say we need to find out if that baby is going to keep us all awake every night or if I'm going to have to blast out one of those tunnels for her to sleep in." They both laughed knowing he was kidding. The walls in the hideout were several feet thick, and they couldn't hear anything between them. It was the perfect setup. They thought if Belle wanted to give them a run for their money and try to keep them awake, she could have at it.

"I think we need to get her completely hidden," Jackson said very seriously. Jude agreed with a nod of her head. Jackson took off his moving gloves and grabbed a bottle of water, leaving a six pack of colas in the fridge. "We can leave all of this as is, as if we're still living at home. The most important thing now is to not leave anything—not even one diaper pin, nothing—to link Jessica and Belle to Aurora."

Jude looked up at him as she put a manual can opener in the last box. "I didn't pick everything up here in her room; I'm just leaving it all like it is now. I haven't had time to clean since Daniel and Spencer moved the girls."

"No big deal, Mom. It's just a few diapers and nobody is coming over, so who cares? We'll leave all of the utilities and cable on. We're just camping out for a few weeks to decide what it really takes to live out there permanently."

"I guess you're right," agreed Jude. "All of this will keep until we can come back for the rest of our things. It's surprising how little value everything you've held dear actually has when you compare it to the safety of the family. Let's get this show on the road." Jackson took one last glance out the front window to make sure that mysterious van wasn't sitting there again, and then he got in on the passenger's side.

"Well?" Jude said, as she shifted into Drive, "you think we can make it out of town without getting caught?" They smiled at each other as they eased down the road and headed towards the highway.

Jude stayed tied up in knots until they were finally on the back country roads leading to Aurora.

With all the road carnage, it was three hours later when they pulled into Daniel's driveway. He and Spencer were both on the porch sitting on the wooden steps. Jude was smiling as she put the car in Park. She couldn't wait to see Daniel. He came down the steps and greeted her with a kiss on the cheek and a warm, immersing embrace. Even under the circumstances of the move, she was excited about them all getting to the hideout.

Daniel explained that he and Spencer wouldn't be coming every day; he wanted to make sure if anybody put a tail on him, it would never lead to Decatur. "Y'all come in and have some tea," said Daniel, taking Jude by the elbow.

"Do we have time, Jackson?" asked Jude, glancing over at her son.

"Yep, we have a bit, and Spencer and I have some things to load in the trunk." The guys disappeared into the barn while Jude and Daniel went in the house.

"Hi, Mom," Jessica said, not getting up. She was nursing the baby and had a diaper thrown over her shoulder and Belle's head for privacy.

"How is my granddaughter?" she asked, sitting next to Jessica on the sofa. She rubbed Belle's little head, but Belle was "on the job" and never even opened her little eyes.

Jude smiled at Jessica and the tender scene. She had never imagined Jessica having a baby, much less agreeing to nurse one. Jessica hoisted Belle up on her shoulder and tapped the age-old rhythm of baby burping until she hit pay dirt.

Daniel came in with a tray holding glasses of iced tea, and they each took one. "Nope," said Daniel to Jessica, shielding the glasses. "The one with the lemon wedge is yours; it's decaf."

Jessica cocked an eyebrow at him and turned to Jude. "He's taking this Dr. business to an unhealthy level—no coke, coffee, chocolate, none of the good stuff."

Jude winked at Daniel and sympathized with Jessica, condescendingly patting her head. "It won't be forever," she said, encouragingly.

"Well, you try going without your two cups a day, Mom; it's no fun."

Jude changed the subject, got up and walked towards Daniel where he was looking out over the yard at the boys loading a couple of farm things into the overcrowded trunk of Jude's car. They stepped out, and Daniel pointed toward the western skies at the storm clouds rolling in. Jude shuddered and rubbed both arms. With all of the smog and ash that hung overhead, it was hard to tell the rain clouds from the soot. Spencer breezed by them and grabbed Jessica's packed items and took them to the car. They were packed and ready to go in half an hour. A part of Jude wanted nothing more than to just stay here with Daniel, but the other part would never choose to be away from her kids or her new granddaughter. They held hands as he walked her down to the car.

Jessica appeared on the porch with a diaper bag slung over her shoulder, and Spencer carried Belle's carseat as if it didn't weigh but two pounds. "Just don't start making baby voices at her," teased Jackson, as he took the baby and tried to figure out how to click in the carrier.

"Move, tattoo boy," said Jessica, as she reached her lanky arm around him and snapped the carrier in snug on the first try.

"Whatever," said Jackson, dryly.

Jessica and Spencer smiled and exchanged glances while Jude got in the driver's seat and started the car. Daniel leaned in for a quick kiss, and Jackson piled in the front after helping Jessica into the overcrowded backseat. They could barely see Belle through the blankets piled around her. Jessica leaned over to her and said, "Can you say 'Hoarders'?" They all broke out in peals of laughter as they pulled away with Jackson humming the theme song of the *Beverly Hillbillies*.

"Time to get serious, guys," said Jackson. "This is no ordinary camping trip. This is the real thing. We're going into hiding the minute we pull off on that dirt road."

Nobody said anything else until they reached their little dirt road. Within no time, they had slipped off the main road and were out of sight. Jackson told them he had a special place to park Jude's car farther in than they normally left them. They had another place deeper in the woods that was a perfect thicket to hide it in.

"Mom, you drive the Jeep and follow me to the car dump. Then I'll ride the rest of the way with you guys."

"So how are we going to get all of our things to the hideout?" Jude wanted to know.

"Don't worry about any of that stuff, Mom. I have a little trailer and a four wheeler at the hideout. I'll come back to get everything."

Before long, they were pulling up at the camp. The ones who had been rescued came out to greet them. They were so happy to see them. Even though they didn't really know each other, there was an air of community among them, and they were so grateful to all be alive and free. After unpacking all of their things in the small east tunnel reserved just for them, Jude was the first to go into the community rooms and start introducing herself.

Sherri was there, and so was the other Sherry and her son, along with three other women, six men and a young lady named Lexy. The group ranged in age from 23 to 68. The 68-year-old woman, Louise, had deemed herself cook, and the others had assigned themselves chores and duties already. Jude instantly felt a connection with the women. She was anxious to see how everything ran and was glad they had all of the kinks worked out before she and the kids ended up going there. She told Louise she liked the idea of camping; it was the reality that liked to rear its ugly head, like bathroom stuff, lack of privacy, wild hogs, possums and such. Louise assured her there were no chamber pots or skinning rabbits.

Jackson checked on Jessica and Belle and made sure they were settling in nicely and then went into the great room to talk to the guys who were milling around waiting for him.

One of the men handed Jackson the journal he had been keeping on everything there from inventory to who had septic duty. It appeared to him it was running smoothly. Jackson called the whole group together, and they decided before they considered themselves in total hiding, they would enjoy an open fire and a sort of "coming in" celebration. That night, they all went outside about 60 feet from the secret door and gathered around a blazing fire with marshmallows on coat hangers, hot dogs threaded on spits and Jude made s'mores for everybody.

Jackson sat with Jude and Jessica on a big blue quilt Jude's mother had made years before. After they ate and laughed and talked, they started exchanging stories about the different arrests that had brought them to the Camp.

It ended up that there were two ministers, an electrician, a plumber, a painter, a cop and an artist among them. Everyone in the little group had had their lives as they had known them, taken from them. They all shared their religious beliefs and said it felt so good to be free and to be able to share their faith openly.

The campfire celebration was short-lived when they began to hear the roar of helicopters! "What?!" shouted Jackson. "This has never been in their flight pattern. What are they doing this far out?"

The cop whispered loudly that it might be a training exercise and they should take cover as they began to see huge spotlights flashing through the thick cover of trees—headed right for them! Jackson grabbed Jude and Jessica, and they hunkered down in the thicket. The guys all worked quickly at putting out the fire and covering it completely with dirt and sod. They even pulled some nearby branches over and covered it all, leaving no trace of evidence they had ever been there. They all rushed around until the helicopters were directly overhead, churning and roaring loudly. They were just a few feet above the trees, and everybody held their breath as they got closer and closer.

The sound of the choppers startled Belle, and she began crying. There was nothing they could do! She cried louder than Jude had ever heard her. All Jessica could do was try to direct her scream into her shoulder. "Oh gosh, Mom," whispered Jessica, "she's going to give us all away!" Jude sheltered them as best she could, and then Jackson put his arms around them all to keep them still. Mercifully, the choppers all flew right on by, never even hesitating.

Jude turned to Jessica and said, "That was her last midnight trip outdoors." Nobody said a word as they all rushed quickly back to the safety of the underground hideout.

The whole group went immediately to their own private quarters, grateful for the hideout and thanking God that He had kept them from being seen. Jackson and Jude went in with Jessica and Belle to make sure they were settled down and had everything they needed. Satisfied, they both went to their own chambers, and Jackson poked his head into Lexy's room to make sure she was okay. She said she was, so he told her goodnight and went to his own room. Each had roughly a 15x15 room with a big bed, dresser, lamps and end table. They selected a man each night to be the watchman from a post they had built several feet from the entrance and high up in an old oak tree covered in thickets and wild plums. It looked like an oversized deer stand with total camo.

Daybreak brought Daniel and Spencer. Jude and Jackson were already milling around on the outside of the hideout, and Jessica was walking around with the baby in tow. Jackson wasn't too crazy about it because that far out in the woods were wild animals, and Jessica and the baby were vulnerable. Not to mention after last night, he was going to have to gently tell her they couldn't put the whole camp at risk. Belle would have to be confined to the hideout. They would take turns watching her so Jessica could get out and get fresh air. And no more open campfires!

Jude brought out coffee for them all, and they made sure they were under the canopy of the trees before they settled on some logs to enjoy the coffee. She noticed Lexy had taken a spot close to Jackson. No more wide open spaces where they could be seen by helicopters overhead. Luckily, they had built the hideout with that in mind. It was very well hidden. Daniel told Jude and Jackson that things were so bad in town now that they were seriously wondering how much longer they could continue to get to the funeral home. Daniel looked concerned as he spoke of it. Jackson noticed that Jessica had been gone quite a while. He got up and took the empty cups and headed back down in the hideout to see if she and the baby had come back yet. Lexy joined him, and they searched the rooms together.

"Look at the pretty flowers, Belle," Jessica said, as she glanced back, wondering if she'd gone too far. Something rustled in the bushes, and she stopped for a second, wishing she would have stayed closer to the camp. She had a pistol tucked in the front of her pants, and she gingerly placed her hand on the smooth handle. Something growled—*"more than one something,"* she thought, as she hurried her footsteps holding Belle tight. She was nearly running as she finally had the courage to glance back, and there they were, close on her heels! Four, medium-sized coyotes were gaining on her, and they looked hungry and out for blood. She was trying to think. If she kept running, they would pounce. She had to turn and face them.

She slipped the black revolver out of her pants, but before she could turn, she heard a ferocious bark and something sprang out of the woods! She turned and saw the huge, black shadow of a German Shepherd in mid-air, and she landed standing between Jessica and the coyote pack. She was twice the size of the largest male coyote. Jessica froze as the coyotes seemed to be sizing up the power of the opponent. She felt cornered but had her pistol drawn and was ready to fire. She aimed at the largest coyote as the big Shepherd continued to stand her ground, and then suddenly lunged at the male. Two more coyotes joined in the attack against the Shepherd! The smaller lunged for Jessica, and she fired! The coyote slid right up to her feet—dead.

Her heart was racing 90 mph as the animals continued to fight in a tangled mass of blood, yelps and snarls. Jessica didn't look back, she just ran—she ran even though the tree branches caught her hair and slashed at her face. She held Belle close to her chest and didn't stop until she slammed right into Spencer. Jackson and the other men just ran right past her wordlessly as she shouted, "Coyotes!"

Spencer took Belle and grabbed Jessica's hand, and they both ran together until they were in sight of the camp. Jude had scrambled up in the watchman's post with Daniel, and they both had their weapons drawn and ready to defend the camp. When they saw the kids, they didn't say a word. They kept their eyes on the surrounding trees and brush until they could tell it was safe.

Spencer took the girls in and got them to their room so they could calm down and clean her wounds. She told Spencer what happened as he cleaned the gash on her cheek. The dog had appeared out of nowhere, and all Jessica could see was a giant shadow as she had leapt to her defense.

Jackson and the others got to where the fight had been. All the coyotes were dead, and they found a female German Shepherd lying in a pool of blood, but still breathing. He gently picked her up. *"She must weigh 120 lbs.,"* thought Jackson, and they started back to the camp. He sent the small band of men out to scout around to see if they could find the owner of the dog or any intruders if they had gotten that far up into their property in case the shot had been heard.

When they got the dog down into the hideout, they could tell she had been greatly cared for until recently. She was unkempt, like maybe an unintended abandoned animal. She had a plain black collar that blended in with her jet black coat. She looked well-fed. They didn't know for sure, but by the looks of things, she had just saved Jessica and Belle's lives. Jackson cleaned her up, and after Daniel came back inside, he stitched up a place on her mouth that one of the coyotes had sunk its teeth into. After some cool water and a few meat scraps, she was up and greeting them all.

She was alarmingly large, but she seemed to be friendly, except, evidently, if there was a coyote close by. She perked up her ears and started sniffing into the air when Jessica and the baby approached.

Jessica looked at Jackson and said, "Is it okay for me to pet her and thank her for watching over me and Belle?"

"I think she's fine. Go ahead; she's awesome," replied Jackson. The dog wagged her massive tail and appeared happy to see Jessica. She whined and circled until Jessica squatted down so she could see for herself the baby was in the blanket. She licked Belle's face before Jessica could react and Belle sneezed.

"Thanks, girl, for being there for me, today. You cast a giant shadow as you leapt through the air to save us. I think we'll call you 'Shadow.'"

Jackson nodded and reached down to pet her head. "That's a cool name, Sis, I like it."

They all agreed Shadow was a great name and then went into the big dining hall to eat the beans and rice Louise had made for lunch. They noticed something odd about Shadow when they made certain gestures. She had reactions to some of them. Jackson noticed when he reached up to rub his bald head, that Shadow heeled. And then if he pointed, she rushed in the direction of his finger, searching and sniffing. They assumed she was a trained canine of some sort. The cop who was there had been out hunting all morning and came into camp. They filled him in on the coyote story. He took one look at Shadow and immediately recognized her collar as one of a trained police officer canine. They were thrilled to have another form of protection—one that could literally smell the enemy coming.

They decided that night to take her out with all the men to search the perimeter and make sure they were still alone after the possibility of someone hearing the gunshot Jessica had fired off. They fanned out in a semi-circle and began to walk. The cop had shown Jackson a couple of commands, and she ended up going with him. They were all in camo and blended in perfectly with the foliage. After an hour, they determined they were still undiscovered and went back to camp.

The next couple of weeks rocked on by with no incidents—Daniel and Spencer coming and going, Daniel and Jude falling deeper in love, and Spencer and Jessica realizing they had something between them. They weren't quite sure what, but they both agreed there was something beginning that was undeniable. Jackson had gotten pretty close to Lexy, too, and had been spotted holding her hand a time or two as reported by Jessica, but he still spent most of the days alone, scouting with Shadow— when he could coax her into leaving Jessica and the baby.

Jude told him she was ready to go get a few more things and turn the utilities off at the Colleyville house and then stay in Decatur on a permanent basis. Daniel and Spencer were going in for a couple of days, too, so Jessica decided to go stay in Aurora while Jackson and Jude spent a couple of days in Colleyville—*if the house was still standing*. With all the bombing and vandalizing, they weren't sure what they were going back to. They piled Shadow in the car with them and headed in. They dropped Jude off, and Jackson rode with Daniel back to Aurora to help decide on food, supplies and ammunition they needed to finish loading from Daniel's barn that they had been using for a storehouse. Jackson decided to brave it and rode on to the funeral home with Daniel while he did some last-minute things before closing for a three-day cemetery cleanup he had fabricated so they could take time off from the funeral home without raising any suspicions.

Jude was happy to be home. Everything was just as they had left it. No vandalism, and the bombs hadn't come as far as her neighborhood.

She walked through each and every room and then went into Grayson's office, and with eyes closed, she slowly breathed in deeply through her nose. The air hinted of old books and still held a very faint scent of his cologne. She went to the kitchen and made herself a cola and some popcorn and watched TV for a bit. She wouldn't pack anything this evening; she would do it all tomorrow or the next day. She just wanted to curl up on the couch until bedtime. After a couple of hours of TV and a two-hour hot bath, she sank down in her oh-so-familiar bed and pulled the soft sheets up to her chin.

Chapter 32

Dead Man Walking

In the soft moonlight, there were the dark silhouettes of forty Suits moving towards the front door. It was midnight when Jude was jolted out of bed by the commotion. She raced down the stairs pulling on her long robe as she got to the door. It was about to come off of its hinges at this point. The Suits were shouting and beating on it. She swung it open, and they knocked her back against the wall as they shoved past her. Guns drawn, they silently ascended the stairs like a moving organism. "Clear!" they whispered, after each room was searched. One of the Suits left in charge of her, screamed in her ear, demanding to know where they all were.

"Where are who?" Jude asked, unconvincingly. The Suit slammed her up against the wall, nearly knocking the breath out of her.

"You better start talking, lady. You have no idea who you're messing with!" he spat out.

She tried to jerk away defiantly from him, but he took his heavy forearm and jabbed it into her chin, forcing her head to one side. She was totally pinned with his knee between her legs, his big belly pressing into hers, completely immobilizing her. Her neck muscles burned like fire as he applied more pressure to her chin.

"They're not here; I don't know where they are," Jude lied, trying to get the words out from underneath the Suit's greasy forearm. She could taste his salty sweat. The pain tore through her neck muscles.

"Speak up!" he shouted, and released her chin, only to grab her face, squeezing it with such force, she tasted her own blood in her mouth. By this time, she was terrified.

The other Suits came barreling down the stairs; they were everywhere. One of them was talking loudly on a cell phone. "Nobody's here but the older broad," he said, glancing over to where Jude was still being held.

"Nope, she ain't here, and neither is the brother," said the Suit. "Yeah, we can wait. You close?"

Five minutes later, Tony walked in the front door with a toothpick in his mouth, wearing jeans, a T-shirt and the same ballcap he always wore. Barely giving her a glance, he walked right past her. She was still standing there with her robe half on and half off. The Suit had her arms pinned behind her. Tony talked in hushed tones to a couple of the Suits and strolled into the kitchen. He opened the fridge, had a look around and popped the top of a can of cola. He took a long swig and threw it on the floor, sending it spewing in all directions as the can spun around and around like a water sprinkler. He stood in the doorway for a moment, leaning on one shoulder, the other hand on his hip and just stared with a dead look in his eyes. He marched over to where she was and unceremoniously grabbed her by the back of the neck, bent her over to the floor beside him and started up the stairs, forcing her to walk still bent over. She had to grab the back of his hand that held her to steady herself. She tripped through the tangle of her own hair. She was half crawling up the stairs.

"Why are you doing this to us, Tony?"

"Shut up, Jude," he spat out. "I'm asking the questions here, today."

He got to Jessica's room and pushed Jude to the floor. She fell on her hands and knees and looked up through her tangled curtain of hair to see what he was doing. She didn't dare move. There were baby things everywhere. He motioned for the Suits to wait in the hall. He looked and touched everything. He picked up an obviously worn T-shirt, then smelled the lid on the bottle of lotion on Jessica's nightstand.

"What's all this?!" he roared, starting to come to a realization. "What are these things?" His voice got louder and louder as he picked up a tiny pacifier and an opened package of newborn diapers. "WHERE IS SHE?" he screamed, at the top of his lungs. "SHE HAD THE BABY?" he roared, as the revelation became clear. "WHERE IS MY SON?"

Jude silently prayed Jackson wouldn't come home during the middle of this! They would unload all forty guns on him. *"Please God,"* she said in her mind, *"please keep my children safe."*

"He's not here, Tony, believe me," she pleaded. "He … he … Tony, he didn't make it." She began to cry. "I'm so sorry, Tony, the baby didn't make it."

"SHUT YOUR MOUTH, JUDE!!! YOU'RE LYING! HE DID MAKE IT! YOU THINK I DON'T KNOW WHAT THIS IS FOR?" He waved the pacifier in her face, and then threw it at her with all of his strength. "Jude," he said, in a scary, quiet voice, as he crouched down next to her and grabbed a handful of her hair, twisting the side of her face up to his. "I swear to you, when I find her …." He wound her hair tighter and tighter as he spoke. "And you can rest assured, I will," he whispered directly into her ear, letting the implication hang in the air. He jerked her all the way down on her back by the handful of hair, his weight crushing her as he toyed with the seams of her robe. "I've got a message for Jackson and Jessica," he spat.

"Tony, please, I don't understand. What have any of us ever done to you? Whatever you're thinking, please don't."

When he finally stood up, she tried to crawl away, but he put his boot on the small of her back and shoved her back down. "Nobody told you to move."

She didn't say anything. She lay perfectly still on the floor on her stomach and didn't look up. Tears stung her eyes as she tried to still her breathing. She didn't know this Tony. She heard him running water in the bathroom. Then he dropped a handtowel on the floor beside her on his way out. The sound of his footsteps got fainter and fainter as he trailed down the stairs. She heard the door slam behind them all.

Jude waited for what seemed like forever, then crept to the top of the stairs to see if they were all gone. As soon as she was sure they were, she fled down the stairs and bolted the door.

Daniel dropped Jackson off at nearly 2:00 a.m. in the morning and drove away, thinking of Jude upstairs fast asleep. Jackson came in quietly through the garage and used his key to come through the laundry room door. He went through the dark kitchen, realizing he was walking in something wet. *"What in the world? Had a pipe burst? Had the dishwasher run over?"* he wondered, and then he turned on the kitchen light and saw the spilled cola all over the floor. He froze. Something wasn't right here. He turned the kitchen light back off and slipped his shoes off, creeping from the dining room to the den.

There was just enough light coming through the window to outline her shape on the sofa. He strained his eyes in the twilight. "Mother? Is that you?" Jude didn't say anything; she just waited. "What's wrong, Mother?" Jude couldn't speak; she dreaded this. He reached to turn the lamp on, and she touched his arm.

"Jackson, I'm okay. Before you turn that light on, I'm okay."

He immediately stiffened up. "What are you talking about, Mother?" His heart began to pump very hard.

"The Suits came while you were gone—and Tony, he came, too."

His hand shook as he switched on the lamp.

She was curled up in a blanket. Her hair was a mess, and she had bruises and scrapes on both arms.

"What's happened here?" he asked, and pulled her face up through the tangle of hair. "Look at me, Mother."

Jude resisted, but he forced her to look up and could instantly see her neck was bruised, there were purple fingerprints on her cheeks and her lips were bruised and bleeding.

You could hear him roar for a city block. "I'm going to KILL HIM!" Jackson stood up, looked down at her and with clenched fists, asked her, "What did he do?"

She grabbed both of his hands, and said, "I'm fine; it's over."

He shook her hands off of his. He was seething with rage. He stood with anger and hatred pooling in his eyes. It was boiling up inside of him like never before. "What did he do?" He shouted, loud enough to shake the rafters: "YOU'RE A DEAD MAN WALKING, TONY! DO YOU HEAR ME? A DEAD MAN WALKING!"

Chapter 33

Dark Was the Morning

Jude said nothing. She waited for him to get a handle on it. He knelt down beside her, heartsick. "Look at your arms, Mother," he said, holding them up. "Are those his handprints on your face?" he asked, between clenched teeth.

"No, one of the Suits did that," she answered lifelessly.

"I'm going after him!" he said, nostrils flaring.

"No, Jackson, you can't go after him. That's what he wants. He will be expecting it. Please, don't leave me here," she pleaded. He stopped cold in his tracks. She was scared, hurt, and all he could think of was killing Tony. There would be time for that. Right now, it was all about her. And she was right. It's what Tony wanted to happen, but they had no idea why.

"I'm not going to leave you," he said tenderly, and helped her up. "Can you walk or do you need me to carry you?"

"No, I can walk."

He got her to her bathroom and turned the bathwater on. "You want any of this stuff in it?" he asked, looking at the different bottles and jars of salts and fragrances.

"No, just get me a bar of soap." He reached under the sink and got it for her. "I thank God you weren't here," she said.

"Well, this night would have ended up a lot different if I would have been," Jackson said.

"That's what scared me," replied Jude.

He shook his head but didn't argue. "I'll be close if you need me. Wanna leave your door open?" he asked.

"No, that's not necessary. I'll be fine."

Jackson went downstairs to clean the cola up. He got out a roll of paper towels and began to soak up the sticky liquid while the theater of his mind rolled the tape.

His phone buzzing on the counter broke his train of thoughts. It was Daniel. "Everybody's sleeping soundly here. It may just be a silly feeling I have, but is everything okay over there?" asked Daniel, as he peeked in on Jessica and Belle. When Jackson hesitated, Daniel said, "You're awfully quiet, Jackson. What's wrong?"

Within two minutes, Daniel was headed back to Jude's. He was fuming—full of fury. *Tony is living on borrowed time. How can I get to him? Tomorrow, I'll dig out my old sniper camo clothes and my "go bag" and pay a visit to that Camp. I'll do things to that man that nobody would think me capable of.* His Special Ops training came back in a flood, and it was all he could do to keep from driving straight through the gates. But he wouldn't; he was older, more disciplined than that. He would bide his time until it was perfect. Besides, getting to Jude was the most important thing now.

He knocked loudly until Jackson let him in. Jude was coming down the stairs, towel-drying her hair. When she saw him, she dropped the towel and ran, falling into his arms. Then she just lost it. He held her right there in the foyer until she finished. "I was so scared *and* angry," she cried. He wrapped his arms around her and took her into the den.

Jackson came around the corner and brought her a cup of tea. "Are you going to be okay, Mom?"

"Yes, I'm getting over the scared, and getting to the angry, part now. I'll get through this, I promise, but why did I ever come back here?" she wondered out loud.

He nodded and said, "I'll sleep by the front door tonight. Daniel, I'll talk to you in the morning." Daniel nodded in agreement and turned his attention back to Jude.

She calmed down, and told him every detail of Tony and the Suits— the way he had treated her, talked to her, everything. She didn't hold anything back.

Jude wasn't his wife, but he had never wanted to hold a woman like he wanted to hold her tonight. He wished he could make her feel safe and loved and protected. There were some things that mere words could not convey. But for now, he'd comfort her within the boundaries of their relationship, and that would have to be enough. And Tony? That guy had a day of reckoning coming, and it was just a matter of who would get to him first—him or Jackson.

Chapter 34

The World as We Knew It

Nobody slept well. Jackson woke up first and came into the den, rubbing his back. Jude's head was slumped over on Daniel's shoulder, both still sitting on the sofa under an afghan, but they had begun to stir.

"Hey, guys, Jessica just called to say there was a loud rumbling going on in Aurora all night and this morning. She said she didn't know if it was the earth or the military base, but it was loud and it was close." Jackson turned on the lamp and saw Jude's face. "Mother, your face is almost totally blue on the left side!" Jude's hand immediately went up to touch it; it was tender. Daniel rubbed his eyes and stood to stretch while Jude excused herself and went upstairs to brush her teeth and inspect her bruises. She was sore all over. She gently washed her face and pulled her hair into a ponytail.

Before long, they were silently sipping coffee at the bar, both men lost in their own thoughts and fantasies regarding Tony's demise, while in the stillness they noticed the rumbling was constant here, too. It was like the earth was moving to the tune of distant thunder. They sat at the bar and decided they should just go—better sooner than later.

The decision was really made last night. She wasn't going to be here when, and if, Tony came back. Something was in the air. Something felt … off. Her intuition was spot on. The city alarms sounded off loudly. They all dashed in to see the broadcast, and there was the White House's Chief of Staff on every network advising all communities to prepare for attack. ISIS cell pods in every city had burst open moments before in New York City, Richmond, Orlando, Chicago, then in Shreveport, Corpus Christi, Dallas, El Paso, Carlsbad, Salt Lake City, Seattle and Los Angeles. Undetected, black submarines had popped up in the oceans and seas and were engaging in open waters with the Navy. Every major city in America was under attack in colossal, organized unanimity.

"Oh, no, guys! We have to go, now!" Jude shouted, "while we can still make it out." Jackson and Daniel rushed around gathering all of the weapons in the house and filled the car. Jude rushed upstairs and threw all she could in a bag. They had to get out of there!

The faithful anchormen blasted the horrors taking place all over the world. It wasn't just in America; it was worldwide. Iran was bombing Tel Aviv, and the earth shook from Jerusalem all the way across the Jordan River. ISIS marched through Bethlehem, desecrating all of the holy sites, while Jews flocked to the Wailing Wall in droves. Every nation was under siege.

A thick cloud of smoke hung overhead, darkening the skies. They all stopped again to listen as the Press Room was gearing up to hear the President speak. Nobody could understand why he hadn't sent the Marines, the Army, Navy or Air Force into the cities to defend the homeland. He wasn't interested in being the Commander-in-Chief; he was no leader. A leader would order troops to start bombing every cell pod in America. He was hunkered down in the White House like a puppet. Americans had taken to the streets with their own arsenals of weapons and were taking out as many of the enemy lines as possible. The more they took out, more seemed to appear out of nowhere. The Armed Forces had pods of their own breaking out against the direct order of the White House Situation Room. There were tanks engaging and hand-to-hand combat everywhere, yet it hardly made a dent.

Within the first hour of the great invasion, every convenience store in every major American city began to blow up simultaneously like bottle rockets, starting at one side of the Continental U.S. to the other. Jude and Jackson rushed around frantically grabbing everything they could as the explosions got closer! They were on the last load when the President came into view. They gathered for the last time around the big screen. He was standing at the podium, but it wasn't the USA flag flying beside him. It wasn't Old Glory for whom over a million soldiers had given their lives for—had bled and died for. It wasn't like what Francis had penned as the rockets lit up the dawn's early light. There were now two black flags with foreign white slashes on either side of him shoved down in the flag barrels of the podium.

The President stood holding his hand up as the roar of the Press Room grew louder and louder in protest. But he couldn't shut this crowd down. He had lost every ounce of credibility all across America. The roar of the press was deafening, and they had actually begun to come out of their seats and were moving toward him until a wave of machine guns silenced them all—permanently!

Jude and the guys stood in complete shock, staring in disbelief at what they had just witnessed, and then they saw "him." In the corner, you could see glimpses of him. The Suits called him "The One." His henchmen flanked both sides—surrounding him, protecting him. He waited patiently in the shadows. The bright lights from the lone, stationary camera that was still rolling, picked up glints and glimmers from his thin golden crown and the curling serpent inlaid with rubies.

"Is that like ... the Antichrist?" Jude said, more than asked.

"It can't be," said Daniel, "or we're all in big trouble."

"That's right," agreed Jackson, "that would have meant we missed the Rapture altogether."

"I know, I know, but this is evil in some form. Is he the False Prophet?" Jude shuddered at her own words.

"I'm not sure who he is, but we aren't going to hang around to find out," yelled Daniel.

They heard a shrill whistle getting closer and closer, and then a deafening explosion as something crashed through the roof, demolishing the entire second floor. It nearly deafened them. Their ears were ringing and they scattered.

"Run!" shouted Jackson. They all bolted out the front door with what they had in their hands, running for the car! Daniel mashed the accelerator as Jude looked back. For a brief moment, she felt like she was in somebody else's body as she watched her house collapse in on itself, leaving a huge black cloud of smoke and fire. She clutched her mother's teacup as the house disappeared behind them forever.

Chapter 35

The Baby

In Aurora, Spencer was out inspecting a suspected leak in the well house, and Shadow had disappeared to go exploring, when the army of Suits pulled up and surrounded the house. A sniper's rifle found Spencer before he could run to warn Jessica. The bullet shattered his clavicle, slamming him to the ground. All he could do was watch from 100 feet away as they stormed the house. Tony glanced around the property one more time before he crushed out his cigarette and opened the screen door.

Jessica was in the kitchen giving Belle a bath in the sink as the Suits descended on her. She stood dumbfounded as they cleared a path for Tony. The washcloth fell out of her hand, splashing over on the baby. She couldn't move her mouth to utter a sound. He closed the distance between them from the door to the island sink and peered down at the baby while he waved a pistol carelessly around. Jessica wordlessly stared up at Tony. When she was finally able to speak, all she could form was his name. "Tony?"

He held up his hand for silence. He pointed into the water, motioning with the gun. "Let me see him. Did you really think you could hide him from me? I've got big plans for him."

"What do you want with us?" she demanded to know. "And I don't know why you keep saying 'him.' You didn't even ask, but the baby turned out to be a girl."

Tony turned as pale as a sheet. "It's a WHAT?" he roared, reaching to snatch the washcloth off Belle.

"Don't hurt her, Tony, please," pleaded Jessica, not understanding his rage. She glanced from the front door to the window. "She's your flesh and blood, Tony! She's just an innocent baby."

"You can stop looking for him, Jessica. I had a sniper trained on your boyfriend long before I got here. He ain't goin' anywhere. He's not going to rush in to save you. He's down at the well house probably choking on his own blood by now."

Jessica screamed for Spencer, but nobody came. "Please, Tony, why are you doing all of this? I don't understand. Why are you so mad at us?"

"It's not about you, you're just collateral damage. It's about the kid. I've promised it to my regime."

"Your WHAT? For what?" Jessica, horrified, struggled to understand.

"You could never understand it," he said, growing agitated. "You people have a book of fairy tales, but it's not like that in my religion. It's a great honor to present our infant children in service of our King—never to be tainted with the tales of your 'Good Book.'"

"A king? What king, Tony? Like in England? You're not making any sense."

"I don't have to make sense," he snarled. "I came here for the kid. Now hand it over. It's time to go; enough of this crap."

Jessica started to back up, clutching the baby. She held on for dear life. He turned toward the Suits. "Y'all can all go now," he motioned to them, "I got this. I thought we'd have more of a 'crowd,'" he said, holding up quote signs with his fingers.

He turned back to Jessica and the baby. "I figured that brother of yours would be here or your new daddy," he spat viciously, "so I brought an army. You know, I came prepared. But as usual," (He raised both hands up, twisting them like he was unscrewing light bulbs, looking around) "he's nowhere to be found—not when I had your mother on the floor, and not now when you need him the most. What a huge disappointment he's turning out to be. Your 'savior' ain't saved anything."

They hadn't told Jessica about what had happened to Jude. They hadn't had a chance. The bile rose in her throat. She just stared at Tony in disbelief. She didn't know this man. But at that moment, she could have sterilized him with her bare hands. "My mother on the floor?" she said, with fear welling up within her. "What did you do to my mother?"

The bombs started getting closer. Things were escalating faster than he had expected. He needed to get back to the Camp. He'd spent enough time here. "Hand her over. I'm not kidding! I swear, I'll rip her from your arms!" He was still holding a gun on her, glancing down at his watch. They were going to gather later to collect gifts for the King. And it may not be as great to give a girl, but he was doing it anyway. He'd already pledged it.

"No, Tony, I can't! Please don't make me! I can't do it. How can you ask me to, Tony? I love her. How will you take care of her or feed her?"

He glanced down and could tell she was engorged with milk. "We'll make do," he nodded. "I see you'll have a reminder for quite a while," he smirked, as he wagged the gun from side to side in front of her chest.

But she still didn't give him the baby. "Please, just let me go with you. I'll do anything you say," she begged.

"JESSICA!" he roared, "give me that kid! If we start wrestling for her," he threatened, "this gun might go off!" He waved it carelessly around. "She could get hurt. For once in your life, woman, just do what I say. Hand her to me."

"Oh, Tony, what's happened to you?"

"I'm more me than I've ever been. I have a purpose now. I'm part of something way bigger than you and your holier-than-thou family."

"Can I at least dress her first?" Jessica pleaded.

Tony raised the pistol. "You're stalling. Cut the crap. I said, 'hand her over.' I'm not asking again."

He came closer, and Jessica, fearing for her baby's life, had no choice. She finally relented and loosened her grip. She didn't want her being hurt during a struggle, but her arms wouldn't let her hand Belle over to him. He'd have to pry her out of her arms. She looked longingly through the window down the long drive, praying she'd see that car turn the corner, but it was nowhere in sight. All she saw was a streak of red as a startled redbird flew from its perch. He grabbed the baby out of her arms, bracing her against his stomach. She was so tiny. She wasn't crying, she was just cooing at her mother's voice as Tony backed towards the door. Jessica whimpered and fell to her knees, inching towards them, holding her arms out as he got closer to the door.

He turned to go out, and that's when he felt the ice cold barrel of the gun between his eyes. "You're not going anywhere with that baby, mister," said Spencer, in a cold, threatening voice. Blood stained his white shirt crimson as his shoddy, medical patch-work bled through. Once he saw the Suits leave, he was able to start making his way across the yard. He had lost a lot of blood. He was pale, but he was standing. Tony put his gun hand on the back of the baby, not hurting her, but showing his capability.

"Back up, little man," said Tony. "I thought you were dead."

"Nope, afraid I can't do that, pal."

Belle had started to whimper with the negative energy flowing through Tony until she heard Spencer's familiar voice and tried to hold her head up towards him and gurgled. Spencer didn't take his eyes off of Tony. He demanded that he put the baby down. Belle was still dripping from the bath and slippery, but Tony held her tight.

"I'll tell you what, little man," he said again, looking up at Spencer, "I'll put her down if you'll put the gun down first. We'll do this another day," he bargained. "I won't shoot you, and you won't shoot me. And the kid can stay here. How's that sound?"

Jessica tried to stand, but instead stumbled. For a split second, Spencer took his eyes off of Tony, and Tony seized the moment. The fire that shot through Spencer's leg as Tony slammed his steel-toed boot into his shin brought him to his knees. Tony grabbed the gun and slid it across the room and with the butt end of his own pistol, cracked Spencer on top of the head. He fell back like a stone. Tony ran out the door and jumped into his van and pealed out in a cloud of dust, slinging rocks everywhere as he slid halfway down the drive. Jessica grabbed up Spencer's gun and ran uselessly behind the car, shooting until the clip was empty.

Chapter 36

Empty Arms and a Rise to Power

It was another 40 minutes before Daniel exited off 287, dodging multiple areas of debris and throngs of people carrying weapons. Country people didn't wait for permission to carry; they were openly patrolling the roads, some with guns and knives, and others with pitchforks and shovels.

They were turning down the half mile driveway of the house when Daniel strained his eyes to see what was ahead. "Who is that? Stop the car!" shouted Jackson. Daniel skidded to a stop, and they all jumped out.

Jackson got to her first and shook her shoulders. "Jessica!"

All she could say was, "Tony." Her feet were bare and bleeding along with both knees as she had fallen on the sharp rocks while chasing the car. Daniel jumped back in the car and floored it, racing the rest of the way up the drive. He was afraid to ask about Spencer, afraid of the answer—but even more afraid of what they would find. He knew if Tony had taken that baby, it had to have been over Spencer's ... he couldn't let his mind go there. He would hold out all hope until he got to him.

Daniel left the car running as he yelled and searched for Spencer. He found him lying crumpled in the doorway right where Tony had left him in a pool of dark red blood with Shadow licking his face. Daniel felt for a pulse. It was faint, but thank God, it was there. He was alive—at least for now. *It's time to take Tony out!*

Daniel got him under his one good arm and dragged him to the sofa. Shadow stood guard as he ran and got his bag and began to tie up the shoulder. He got the blood flow stopped, cleaned his head where the pistol had laid it open and made a makeshift splint for his broken shin bone. He thanked God for his son's hard head; it may have just saved his life. When Spencer started coming in and out of consciousness, Daniel spoke softly to him, encouraging him to be still. He was fighting and clawing, trying to grasp something. "Spencer, you're safe. It's Dad. Wake up, son. He took the baby, but we won't rest until she's home."

Fifteen minutes later, Daniel and Jackson were headed to the C-Camp with Jude in the backseat. She blatantly refused to stay behind. She wanted Tony's blood as much as they did. Jessica was left to care for Spencer until they got back. She knew Jackson wouldn't leave without Belle; he promised her. They all had.

The President turned the microphone over to the King. He had a deep, resonating, enticing voice and told the world that he had come to bring peace; had come to restore world order. He had come to make all things new. He spoke blasphemies to every nation and every tribe. The world was mesmerized by his soothing words. He called for an immediate ceasefire and invited all world leaders to come together immediately at the United Nations where he would lay out the plan to restore world order and peace to all mankind. He instructed the General Assembly as well as the Security Council to fly in to the headquarters in Nairobi (Kenya) instead of Manhattan, as it lay in ruins.

The Presidential procession carried him to a private airport where he boarded Air Force One which was cleared for takeoff and taxiing down the runway in a matter of minutes.

Chapter 37

Tony, Where Art Thou?

With all the cities burning, debris everywhere and the smoke-filled air, it took hours to get to the Camp, but they did. They got within half a mile of the main gates and pulled off down past a patch of trees and vines. They hid the car behind some bushes and gathered their supplies.

Daniel had full-on camouflage and his "go bag" slung across his back. Jackson was in a tanktop and the rest full-on camo and had strapped on an extra 100 rounds of ammunition to his waist belt. Jude followed silently behind them with two .38 revolvers stuffed in her belt, and she was carrying Grayson's old shotgun. They stopped silently in the woods and smeared mud on their faces to eliminate any glare. As they got close, they could see part of the Camp fence had been blown up, leaving a hole in the wires.

They all crouched low and made it to an outcropping of rocks within 25 feet of the breach. Jackson squatted down and pulled Jude down beside him. "Mother," he whispered, motioning with his head, "go up in those rocks, watch for snakes, get comfortable and don't take your eyes off of the fence. You have plenty of ammunition and a clear view. Don't come across that fence line! No matter what happens, you stay put and don't make a move until you see the whites of my eyes." Jude nodded her head in agreement and grabbed his hands as he started to stand. She looked up into those eyes, and they locked for a brief moment, and they both nodded.

Then she turned to Daniel as Jackson crawled about five feet away to get a closer look. Daniel crouched down beside her on one knee and cupped her cheek and looked deep into those green eyes. He kissed her sweetly and whispered, "Just in case I don't make it out of here, I want to tell you something."

"Don't talk like that, Daniel," she pleaded, putting her hand on his cheek. "I can't handle that. You're going to make it out—we all are."

He put his fingers on her lips. "Shhh. Let me say this. I want to tell you that I love you ..." (He looked deep into her eyes and could barely get the next words out.) "like I've never loved another woman. Jude Mitlow, if we make it out of here alive, would you be willing to spend the rest of your life with me?"

Jackson, on his belly, jerked his head around. "You gotta be kidding," he whispered. "If we ever get out of here, I need to talk to you about your timing."

Jude smiled at Daniel's muddy face, and he smiled back at hers. It was perfect timing for her. "I love you, too, and I can't think of anything I'd love more," she said. "Now, go get that baby!" He grabbed her, and they held each other tight.

She didn't have to tell them twice. Within seconds, they crawled through the opening of the fence and disappeared into the thicket from her view. Jude positioned herself behind the rocks and prayed for safety. She fixed her eyes on the fence, and that's when she saw it—a beautiful redbird perched on the jagged, broken fence. At every turn in her life, it had always been a sign for her. Like beauty in the ashes, she saw the contrast of bright red against the smoky desolation. She knew God was with them; and she bet before this day was over, Tony would be wishing the same thing.

Daniel and Jackson both had their backs up against opposite walls. They had made it to the barracks.

Daniel saw Bob and Liz creeping through the alley. "Bob!" Daniel whispered, and got his attention. They glanced around and silently slipped over and flattened out against the wall with him. They noticed Jackson directly across from them against the wall, catty-cornered from the officers' bunkhouse. Bob and Liz could barely recognize them in their garb and muddy faces; they both looked like something out of a

Stallone flick. Bob held up two fingers on each hand like a crewman bringing in a plane, and motioned for them to give him time to get the doors unlocked. He had keys to every building. He whispered to Daniel that he'd take care of any guards in the halls, as he squatted down and gathered mud for his own face; he was all in at this point. Daniel slipped him a sharp hunting knife. Bob nodded; the gun would give them all away. He slipped it in his boot. "Take care of Liz should this thing head south," he whispered, as he darted across the alley.

Daniel told Liz exactly where the fence had been breached and how to get there. They all watched as Bob made it to the officers' private entrance and stuck the key in the hole. "Don't let anyone follow you, Liz. It'll mean certain death for all of us," Daniel whispered.

"Not a chance," she said, as ice water ran through her veins. She had no idea until he told her that it was Jude's grandbaby who had been kidnapped and brought here. She had heard a baby crying, off and on, all day.

"Jude will see you when you get close to the hole in the fence," he whispered. "Be careful; she may not recognize you at first." Liz nodded. Daniel turned to watch Bob as he disappeared into the hall. When he looked back to tell Liz that Bob was in, she had already slipped away.

Once Bob had the hallway cleared, he motioned for Daniel and Jackson to come on. They looked both ways and silently crossed the gap and closed the door behind them. There were two guards already lying with their throats cut, and they could see Bob dragging a third one down into another hallway. He'd made good use of the knife.

Daniel crept along the dark wall with stealth-like movements, making his way to the officers' quarters. His job was to take the whole division out. Jackson's job was Tony. They got closer to the bowels of the dark bunkers. Bob silently followed Jackson until they got to the main hall. Then he signaled which door was the interrogation room. He wiped the sweat and blood splatters off of his glasses and slipped away to join Daniel.

Daniel had already taken out the four officers in the mess hall and was going room to room to find the rest. They all stopped in their tracks as they started hearing gunfire on the outside of the bunker. Two officers came barreling in out of nowhere as Daniel motioned for Bob to take cover. They both hid behind an Army green laundry cart as the officers filed by. Daniel slipped up behind them and slammed their heads together, knocking them out stone cold, then finished the job. Bob, pushing the rickety laundry cart, met Tony as he darted in carrying what they presumed to be the baby. She wasn't making any sounds. Bob just stood up and blocked his way as he tried to move around the cart.

"Who the Sam Hill are you?" asked Tony, as he reached for his gun.

"Your worst nightmare," Daniel whispered loudly, as he popped out of the laundry cart and smashed Tony's forehead with the butt of his gun. Tony staggered forward, and Daniel relieved him of the baby before he fell backwards—out cold, still wearing his mirrored sunglasses.

Bob started to pick up Tony's feet to drag him out when they both spotted Jackson coming through the hall. He was puffed up and walking with determination. He saw Daniel with the baby and checked on her first. "You ready to go home, Tinker Belle?" he said, covering her belly with his hand. She cooed at the familiar voice, but they had a job to finish. They each straddled a mess hall bench until Tony started coming to. He was lying on the floor in the middle of them. They had formed a circle around him. Bullets were whizzing all around the building, but they still took their time. Tony wasn't going anywhere, and neither were they. It was time Tony paid the piper.

Daniel grabbed a bucket of ice cold water and threw it in his face. He gasped and tried to sit up, but Jackson stood up and said, "Get on your hands and knees."

Tony, feeling trapped and still a little woozy, staggered onto his hands and knees. "What are going to do to me, pervert?" Daniel and Bob looked at each other but didn't say anything.

Tony defiantly started to get up anyway and Jackson, with his boot, shoved him back down.

"Is that the way you did my mother, Tony?"

Tony turned over and met Jackson's eyes with hatred. "You really want to know about me and your mother?"

Jackson didn't wait for another word. He kicked him in the head, knocking him back out. He picked up one boot like he didn't weigh anything and started dragging him down the hall. Bob darted in front of him and opened the door of the interrogation room where he and Liz both had been held from time to time. Jackson dragged him in and dropped his leg on the dirt floor. His pants were half down by now. Daniel threw another bucket of ice water in his face, and he started waking up again. Daniel dug his boot into his clavicle and Tony groaned. Jackson waited for him to get good and awake and said, "You got anything else clever to say, little man?"

Tony tried to smile and reach for his pants, but Jackson grabbed him by the face, squeezing it until Tony could taste his own blood in his mouth. He grabbed him by the back of the neck and bent him over and marched him to the chains fastened into the wall. Tony had to grab the back of Jackson's hand to keep from falling as he tripped over his sagging pants that were nearly down around his knees by this point. Bob moved silently forward without any instructions and stretched Tony's arms out good and tight and fastened the chains around each wrist. He nodded at the role reversals here as he removed Tony's sunglasses from him and slipped them into his pocket.

Bob leaned back against the wall with Daniel and quickly cleaned his glasses; he didn't want to miss a thing. "You want me to take the baby out?" Bob asked, in the dimly lit room.

"Nope," Jackson shook his head, "she's not leaving my sight."

"You sure she's not YOUR actual kid?" Tony said. But before he could even get a smirk on his face, Jackson smashed his fist so far into his mouth, he crashed through tissue and bone. Those were the last words that ever came out of Tony's mouth—ever again!

Liz got close to the opening of the fence and spotted Jude. She didn't want to get shot, so she quickly ripped the end of her filthy T-shirt off and tied it to a stick. She belly crawled through the brush on to the dirt gully leading through the opening. She raised it about a foot in the air. She wanted Jude to see it, but not alert every Suit in the compound. Jude had her eyes glued to the breach in the fence. She squinted for a second. *Is that a flag? Is this a trick?* She looked down the barrel of the shotgun, her hand on the trigger. No, nobody knew she was there except Jackson and Daniel. Neither of them, even by torture, would disclose her whereabouts. Jude hesitated, and then she saw who it was—it was Liz! She gave a little "come here" hand motion, and Liz crawled through the opening and scrambled up to Jude's hideout. They grabbed each other and quietly celebrated Liz's escape, but then quickly took their places to "man" the escape hole. Jude handed Liz one of her revolvers and a box of bullets and whispered, "Do you know how to use a gun?"

Liz was already tearing the box of ammo open with her teeth. "Absolutely," she said, never taking her eyes off the fence. She was locked and loaded.

"Let's go," said Daniel, "the gunfire's getting closer. We don't want to be trapped in here like sitting ducks."

They went the way they came in, but when they cracked the door open, there was a problem. There were Suits and Uniforms everywhere. Citizens had stormed the front gate, coming to liberate the prisoners. The Suits were taking heavy gunfire.

"Y'all run! I'll cover you," whispered Bob, as he checked the rounds of ammo in his pistol.

"We can't do that!" said Jackson.

"We're all getting out of here, Bob," said Daniel, as he positioned himself. "You and I will make a path for Jackson and Belle." He pointed with two fingers to where the breach was and whispered, "Now once we start, don't stop until we're at that fence." Bob nodded and Jackson jerked a suit coat off of one of the dead guys and wrapped the baby in it. He cradled her in one arm and positioned the machine gun in the other.

Daniel whispered to them as he quietly opened the door. "On my count of three." He held up his fingers and wordlessly counted them off: "One, two, three." They ran, darting in and out of the barracks, trying to draw the fire their way so Jackson could make a clean run with the baby. They ran shooting and rolling and zigzagging, trying to dodge the shower of bullets whizzing by. Bob took one to the shoulder, and Daniel took a flesh wound to the side of his head, but they kept running! For Jude! For Spencer! For Jessica! For Belle! For Liz! For Freedom! They ran until they could see the hole in the fence. Daniel made it first, sliding and smashing into the fence and quickly turned and held off enemy fire while Bob slid in behind him.

Jude and Liz suddenly fired from their position as an off-road camo Jeep crashed through the brush, full of Suits firing automatic weapons and handguns. The Suits closed in on Jackson as he tucked the baby in like a football and ran faster than he ever had! He put the automatic backwards over his shoulder and just held the trigger down, mowing them down behind him as Daniel and Bob pulled back the wire fence as wide as they could get it. They fired until all you could see was a cloud of smoke and a blaze of glory as Jackson slid through on both knees with his head behind him, covering Belle with both arms. Daniel pulled the pin on his only hand grenade. His aim was true as the camo Jeep exploded into a million pieces! They all scrambled to Jackson as he fell forward, with Jude running and sliding down from the rocky outcrop trying to reach him. He wasn't moving. They thought he was dead. Blood was oozing from three different bullet holes.

"Jackson!" she screamed, scraping up her arms as she slid. She couldn't feel anything. She had to get to Jackson.

Daniel held up his arm and said, "Wait, Jude, please."

"No!" Jude screamed, as she fought her way around him and knelt beside Jackson, struggling to turn him over. With the strength that comes with fear, she turned him over on her own, and there she was, safe in the shelter of his arms. They opened up the suit coat, and she looked up at them with her own dirty little face. He had smeared mud on her, too. But she was unharmed. Jude quickly handed her to Liz and cradled Jackson's head, wiping the dirt and blood off of his face. He was bleeding from several bullet holes, and Jude tried to keep the blood from coming out, her hands going from one wound to the other.

Daniel rushed over. They couldn't tell if Jackson was dead or alive. All of a sudden, his body arched, and he gasped for air! Daniel leapt forward, and together, they got him sitting up. Daniel could now tell the wounds were not fatal. "Are you okay? Can you stand?" he asked him.

"Yeah, help me up. I can make it. That last shot I took knocked the wind out of me." Daniel nodded and put his arm around him and pulled him up. Once he got his bearings, he took Belle from Liz and cradled her in his arms, and they all disappeared out of sight through the woods and made their way back to the hidden vehicle. Daniel got everybody's bleeding stopped and quickly patched before leaving. They dodged several roadblocks and pockets of militia as they drove through the tangled webs of once familiar streets that had been blown to bits. It all looked like a war zone now. Daniel maneuvered the car in and out and even drove off into the ditches when he had to, but he had to get back to Aurora.

"Spencer," he said aloud, randomly. Jude, from the middle of the backseat, still holding hands with Liz, leaned up and put her hand on his shoulder. He put his hand on hers, and they looked at each other through the rearview mirror the rest of the way home. They were all solemn in the car as they thought of Spencer and Jessica. They had left Spencer in quite a mess. With all the explosions, raids and ISIS cell pods, they didn't know what to expect—didn't know if the war had reached their little town and Daniel's house, even though it was hidden from the main roads. Jude had one hand on Daniel's shoulder and now the other on Jackson's. Her heart was so full. They had been in the jaws of death today, but they had come out on the other side together. Their faces were grim as they rounded the final corner to the magnolia-lined drive and the house was in sight.

JUDE

Chapter 38

A Sight for Sore Eyes

Jessica ran to the porch as soon as she heard the car. Jackson opened the car door and stood up holding sweet little Belle. Jessica scrambled off the porch and ran to them. Shadow nearly knocked them all down trying to get to the baby. "I told you I'd bring her back, Sis," Jackson said, as Jessica took her daughter in her arms—laughing and crying at the same time.

They all hugged each other in a family circle while Daniel ran past them to get in the house to Spencer. He threw the door open and froze. Spencer sat there with a huge grin on his face. "Dad, you're a sight for sore eyes."

Daniel rushed over to him, and they embraced each other. He clapped him on the back, forgetting about his gunshot wound—heck, almost all of them had them at this point! He even thought he had seen a bullet hole in Liz's pants.

"Easy, Dad," Spencer said, grimacing and getting lightheaded. "Remember, I've got a busted flipper and a broken leg." Daniel apologized but continued to fuss over his boy. He was never happier to see him at any other time in their lives that he could remember.

Daniel told all the wounded ones to come in the kitchen, and he took turns lovingly binding their wounds. They were home now—even if only for the night. The battle wasn't here but would be within a couple of days.

Later that evening, they made sandwiches out of what they had left at home, and Daniel showed Jude and Jackson around. It was a huge, beautiful Victorian farmhouse near a pond that sat on a sprawling 100 acres and had been in Daniel's family for several generations. Jude and Daniel walked through the barns and then down to the edge of the beautiful, almost translucent pond. They sat under the trees on a blanket and watched as the sun went down, fading from bright golden orange to a pale pink through the smoky horizon, then finally giving way to sketches of moonlight. The crickets were chirping and the frogs were croaking beneath the trees before they made it back to the house. They all slept in peace that night, but the rumbling was growing closer and closer.

The next morning, as they gathered around the breakfast table, Daniel said grace. Jude and Daniel had cooked the only things left in the cupboards. They made biscuits and gravy, along with pancakes and bacon. And there were leftover pork chops and some green beans from a couple of days ago. It was the last of the food here in the house. They ate while they discussed the move to Decatur and how God had seen them safe thus far; and they knew He wouldn't leave them now. Bob and Liz came in and joined them and filled their plates, too. It was good to be free!

Jude glanced over at the kitchen window, and low and behold, a beautiful cardinal sat on a crepe myrtle branch just outside of the window while the wind chimes danced in the gentle morning breeze. She could see Shadow running towards the porch where she had put down a fresh bowl of water for her. She looked at Jackson, Jessica and the new baby and smiled. Jackson squeezed her hand. She looked over to see Daniel putting gravy on Spencer's biscuits and knew in her heart that as long as they were all together, they were as strong as any three-strand cord.

As Air Force One took off from an airport in Nairobi, Kenya, it soared high above the clouds with the King settling in for the long journey home; he was coming back.

The earth began to shake and the hills began to collapse on one another. The rivers and streams gave up their waters as tsunamis gathered in all of the oceans. The earth burst open along every fault line, and the California coast completely disappeared. South America sank into the seas and Alaska moved inland. The earth creaked and the mighty mountains trembled. Creation groaned as earth belched up its core. Volcanos erupted everywhere, spewing volcanic ash seven miles into the morning sky as the lava and magma moved miles toward the cities, destroying everything in its path. Every high-rise in New York City came crashing down, and Florida was completely wiped off the map. The earth split apart in so many cities that the cemeteries unearthed their buried dead. The ground began to shake at the Eternal Rest Cemetery. The rocks rattled, and the pebbles moved across the roads as massive oak trees pushed up until their roots were laid bare. Grayson's grave, like many others, had pushed up and burst open. But something strange had happened—his casket was empty! His body wasn't there!

The breakfast table was still set, and the smoke was still rising from the plate of hot pancakes Jude had just set on the table—but there was nobody there to eat them! There was a robe on the floor between Daniel's and Jackson's empty seats. Jackson's tank top was still floating down to the bottom of his chair. A little, empty diaper, with the tape still fastened, lay in between Jessica's and Spencer's places. There was no sign of Bob or Liz, and a large, black collar lay beside the bowl of water on the porch. The King had indeed come back! The one true King! THE KING OF ALL KINGS! Like a thief in the night, the trumpet had sounded, and He had come and taken them home, just like He said he would.

The End

Or is it really just the beginning?

1 THESSALONIANS 4:16–17 (KJV)

For the Lord himself shall descend from the heaven with a shout, with the voice of the archangel, and with the trump of God; and the dead in Christ shall rise first; then we which are alive and remain shall be caught up together with them in the clouds, to meet the Lord in the air; and so shall we ever be with the Lord.

Epilogue

The grass was never greener, nor the skies ever bluer than they were in that beautiful city. There was no need for the moon or the sun, for the light that shown around them was pure and white. It was the light of the Savior of the World. Streams of glory radiated all around Him. He was, and is, and ever shall be the Lion of the Tribe of Judah, the Great I AM, the Rose of Sharon, the Prince of Peace, Bethlehem's Son, God's Son—Jesus.

Jude, Daniel, Jackson, Jessica, Spencer and little Belle were standing with Grayson, Jude's Mother and Daddy, as well as all of their brothers and sisters. The rest of their beloved family and throngs of friends were gathered around them. But they weren't finished; this wasn't the end.

And there was a new heaven and a new earth with beauty and blessing and indescribable joy. And there the lion did lay down with the lamb. Gold and pearl, sapphires and jasper, and multitudes of angels crying, "Holy, holy, holy, is the Lord God Almighty!" And they all lived happily ever after!

About the Author

Christine Best has written mostly poetry and plays over the years; however, JUDE is her first finished novel. She has three other novels in the making and loves to write. Her background is in bookkeeping and longtime, freelance services at local funeral homes. Her education is a hodgepodge of general studies at a local college, Bible college courses taken online, as well as a background and licensed in real estate and insurance. She is retired from all of her jobs except her favorite job of all—being the best wife, mother, stepmother, grandmother, aunt, sister, daughter, mother-in-law, sister-in-law, niece, cousin and friend that she possibly can be. JUDE was born out of her love of family, survival scenarios and End-Time biblical prophecies.

Contact Information

Email: cbestc21@hotmail.com
Facebook: Christine Blevins Best

www.ingramcontent.com/pod-product-compliance
Lightning Source LLC
Chambersburg PA
CBHW070612130626
46556CB00001B/340